Greenback

Steven Glazer

Published by Steven Glazer, 2025.

This is a work of fiction. Similarities to real people, places, or events are entirely coincidental.

GREENBACK

First edition. January 2, 2025.

Copyright © 2025 Steven Glazer.

ISBN: 979-8230833628

Written by Steven Glazer.

Table of Contents

To my aunt Judith Cabaud

My first muse

$$$$ GREENBACK $$$$
A Novel

By Steven A. Glazer

TABLE OF FIGURES

———

Figure 47: "First Reading of the Emancipation Proclamation by President Lincoln," painting by Francis B. Carpenter, 1864 (PD). Tellingly, Chase and Stanton are to Lincoln's left and the rest of the Cabinet (Welles, Smith, Seward, Blair, Bates) are to his right.

Figure 48: The Past and the Future, by Thomas Nast, 1863 (PD)

Figure 49: General Joseph Hooker

Figure 50: Kate Chase

Figure 51: General Ambrose Burnside (PD)

Figure 52: Secretary of State William H. Seward

Figure 53: Government Buildings for "Contrabands" on Hilton Head, South Carolina (PD)

Figure 54: "Running the Machine," political cartoon by John Cameron, 1864. Chase's successor as Treasury Secretary, William P. Fessenden, is "running" Chases "patented" Greenback machine. (PD)

Figure 55: William and Kate Sprague, photo by Mathew Brady (PD)

Figure 56: Kate Chase Sprague visiting Gen. J.J. Abercrombie at the battlefield defenses of Washington, D.C., circa 1863

Figure 57: Senator Samuel Pomeroy of Kansas (PD)

Figure 58: Thurlow Weed (PD)

Figure 59: Nettie, Salmon, and Kate Chase

Figure 60: Chief Justice Chase's Supreme Court, February 1867 (PD)

Figure 61: Chief Justice Chase

Every law on the statute book so wrong and mean that it cannot be executed, or felt, if executed, to be oppressive and unjust, tends to the overthrow of all law, by separating in the minds of the people, the idea of law from the idea of right.

Salmon P. Chase[1]

—————————

PART ONE
CHASE

———

Chapter One – Don't You Know Who I Am?

⸻

M Y NAME IS SALMON PORTLAND CHASE. I invented money.

Figure 1: Salmon Portland Chase, circa 1862 (PD)

Well, yes, I am only kidding.

I didn't *invent* money. That happened long before anyone ever wrote anything about it. I *did*, however, invent a *kind* of money that we in the United States of America use today. It is made of paper, not metal, and it is backed by ... well, nothing. Nothing except a law that says that you must consider it to *be* money.

More of that later. Right now, let me tell you more about me. It so happens that I have been enormously important to these United States of America.

Figure 2: The Salmon P. Chase Birthplace in Cornish, N.H. (© Jerrye and Roy Klotz, MD, by SA 3.0 Deed)

I was born on Wednesday, January 13, 1808, in the town of Cornish, New Hampshire. Cornish is a small village that at the time of my birth was in Cheshire County, but now is part of Sullivan County.[2]

My father and mother were Ithamar Chase and Jannette Ralston Chase, originally from Keene, New Hampshire.[3] I was the eighth of their eleven children.

When I was eight years old, our family moved from Cornish to Keene and moved into the house of my grandfather, Alexander Ralston.[4] My father quickly became an important figure in Keene – he joined the Masons and enjoyed a close friendship with Congressman Daniel Webster of Massachusetts. Father used a small inheritance that my mother had received to establish a glass factory, but business failed after the conclusion of the War of 1812 put an end to America's high tariffs that had protected entrepreneurs like him from British competition.[5]

About a year after we moved to Keene, Father had a stroke and died. [6] Mother received only a small sum from the remains of the estate. She moved our family out of Grandfather's home into a smaller house in Keene.[7]

In the three remaining years that I lived there, much happened. My eldest sister was married in that house in 1818, and my sixteen-year-old brother Dudley left from there to go to sea. He wrote us letters from his voyages all over the world. Sadly, we learned after two or three years that he had left the ship and died in South America. He was the first of my siblings to pass away.[8]

I spent much of my time in Keene at the Latin school that Colonel Dunham ran in nearby Windsor. He had formerly published a local newspaper called the *Washingtonian*, and I found yellowing copies of his work in crates in his attic. I read them with great interest. The Colonel had been quite the Federalist in his day, and was not too fond of Thomas Jefferson's protégé, James Madison.[9]

I was an assiduous student at Colonel Dunham's school. I studied the Latin classics and was considered by the teachers to be a prodigy. Reverand Barstow taught me Greek and the mathematics and logic of Euclid.[10] Unlike other students, I was good at memorization and thus did not have to reason things out much. I did rather well in these lines of study.[11]

When I was twelve years of age, my uncle Philander Chase came east from Ohio to visit. He was the Episcopal Bishop of Ohio. One day on his visit, he sat down with Mother and had a talk with her. I was in the next room, and when I realized that they were talking about me, I hid behind the wall near them to listen.

"Jan," he said, "Salmon is a truly remarkable boy. I am very impressed with his love of learning."

"He is indeed an amazing boy, Philander," Mother replied. "I hear from the schoolmaster that his mastery of Greek and mathematics is far above average, even for boys who are two years older than he."

"This may sound presumptuous of me, sister, but I am inspired to make a great request of you. Will you allow me to take Salmon west back to Worthington to study at my school there? I am convinced that it will greatly open his mind and impel Salmon to do great things with his knowledge."

Mother was shocked. "Philander, how can you expect me to allow Salmon, at his age, to travel to Ohio, so far from home, to enroll in school? Many children leave home for college, but only at a much older age."

"I *am* a man of the cloth, and I promise you that I will look after his interests assiduously."

There was a long silence. Finally, I heard Mother say, "Well, all right, Philander, you may take Salmon with you to Ohio, if he agrees to go. I expect you to treat him like your own son, of course, and to see to his feeding, housing, and clothing. I have nothing to pay you with, brother, so you must be prepared to take on this responsibility."

"If I *agree* to go?" I thought as I listened. I was already convinced! Uncle Philander was going to take me to Ohio! What an adventure it would be!

I readily accepted and, with Mother's blessing, I accompanied Uncle Philander on the arduous journey west in 1820.[12]

- $ $ $ -

- $ -

At Uncle Philander's school I studied more Greek. I even gave an oration in Greek on a comparison of Peter and Paul, of which both the Bishop and I were very proud.[13] When not in school, I did chores that Uncle Philander assigned to me – taking grain to the mill and returning with the meal or flour; milking the cows, driving them to or from the pasture; bringing wood into the house for the winter; making maple-sugar, planting and reaping; in short, all that a boy of my age at the time might do on a farm.[14]

Uncle Philander's role as Bishop of the Episcopal Church of Ohio did not earn the family much revenue. Worthington, on the northern edge of Columbus, was a poor rural village in the middle of the new state. Most of the church members were farmers, and prices for farm produce was very low. There were no good roads and no accessible markets for their goods. Uncle would say on occasion that his whole monetary income as a bishop did not pay his postage bills. Not surprising, considering that it cost a bushel of wheat to pay for the conveyance of a letter over one hundred sixty miles![15]

While living and working in these stressful circumstances, Uncle was offered the presidency of Cincinnati College in 1822. That

November, the family and I moved to that city and I enrolled as a freshman at the College at the age of fourteen.[16]

My erudition at the College was so outstanding that I advanced by extra study into the sophomore class in my first year. But my college friends in the class did not make study quite as primary an aspect of their lives as I did. Fun and mischief prevailed.

One morning, Dr. Slack, our dean, entered chapel for morning prayers, only to find a stuffed owl standing on the pulpit, wearing a pair of spectacles much like his own! Dr. Slack ever so calmly removed the owl from the pulpit and proceeded with the service, without a hint of the explosion that we boys all eagerly awaited.[17]

I had little or nothing to do with these activities. I preferred reading in my spare time, and meditating on religious topics. I had a strong sense of religious obligation and responsibility.[18] This predilection occasionally got me into trouble anyway.

One day, a fellow sophomore set fire to one of the desks in the classroom just before the tutor arrived. I tried to put the fire out, but it was still burning when the tutor arrived. He put the fire out and directed us to take our seats.[19]

The tutor then walked to the last desk in my row; mine was the first in the row. He questioned the student there: "Sophomore, did you set fire to the desk?" "No, sir," was the reply. "Do you know who did?" he next inquired of him. "No, sir," came the reply.[20]

He moved up the row and eventually reached the culprit. "Did you set fire to the desk?" "No, sir," came the unabashedly false reply. "Do you know who did?" "No, sir," the culprit lied again.[21]

The tutor finally reached me. I was determined to tell the truth, but I could not reveal the culprit for in my mind that would be as evil as lying itself.

"Sophomore Chase, did you set fire to the desk?"

"No, sir."

"Do you know who did?"

"Yes, sir."

The tutor's eyes widened and he bent down to position his nose directly across from mine.

"Who was it?"

"I shall not tell you, sir."[22]

The tutor sprang up straight, cocking his eyebrows in confusion. He said no more and went to the head of the classroom to begin the day's lessons.

I later heard that the faculty had discussed this incident at length afterwards. They decided, however, that it was not worthwhile to convene an inquiry.[23] I have thought many times of that episode in my early life, particularly since I have matured as a lawyer and politician. That was the first time that I used my innate sense of logic to extricate myself from a sticky situation, and my comeback deterred condign punishment. As I will show here eventually, that skill has oft come in handy.

- $ $ $ -

- $ -

I studied at Cincinnati College for a little less than a year. Uncle Philander despaired of his position heading a college in such a poor diocese of the church, and wanted instead to start a theological seminary for educating young men for the ministry, *as well as* a college. He determined to go to England to enlist the help of the church elders themselves. And so, he resigned the presidency of the College and transported himself, his family, and me to Kingston, New York. There I parted from the family and I, then a mere lad of fifteen years of age, made my way east on foot back to my mother's house in Keene.[24]

Chapter Two – Keene To Dartmouth To Washington

───

I WAS OVERJOYED TO SEE MOUNT Monadnock on the horizon, signifying the end of my journey home to Keene. I entered the little yellow house and was greeted by my surprised and joyous mother and sisters. It was good to be back![25]

Figure 3: Mount Monadnock, near Keene, N.H., in young Salmon Chase's Day (Life of Chase, at 16-17)

It was not long before I was again engaged in scholarly pursuits, this time with remuneration. At the age of sixteen, I was hired as a schoolmaster for eight dollars a month in the nearby town of Roxbury and boarded with a farmer there.[26]

I was determined to be a good tutor, but my young age proved to be an impediment to my control over students the same age as myself. I resolved to rectify this imbalance by maintaining a good offense as the best defense. So, when one older boy attempted to bully me, I punished him.

It was no more than two weeks into my job there when I was told by the school board on behalf of the boy's parents that my services were no longer needed.[27]I learned then and there that good offenses often get you fired.

Following that unpleasant attempt at the profession of teaching, I applied for admission to the junior class of Dartmouth College in Hanover, New Hampshire. I was examined by the faculty and admitted in 1824. Following my first term there, I sought another school to manage, and was employed by one in Roxbury, Vermont. That, fortunately, was a greater success than my experience in Roxbury, New Hampshire. I returned to Dartmouth for the new term, adequately paid.[28]

I graduated a year later, and ranked eighth in my class. I was admitted to Phi Beta Kappa Society with the uppermost third of my senior class.[29] After Dartmouth I headed south to Philadelphia to meet up again with Uncle Philander, who had returned from England and was now engaged on behalf of the elders of the church in founding Kenyon College in central Ohio.[30]

Figure 4: Bishop Philander Chase, circa 1824 (PD)

After a short stay with Uncle, I traveled around Maryland in search of a school to administer, but without success. By 1826, I decided to try my luck in the Nation's Capital, Washington City in the District of Columbia.[31]

Although I was well-equipped with letters of introduction from two elders of the Episcopal Church, I found it hard to find employment in Washington. Accordingly, I placed an advertisement in the *National Intelligencer* of December 23, 1826, announcing over my signature that on the second Monday of the following January, I would open, in the western part of the city, a "select classical school" to be available for not more than twenty students.[32]

The response was underwhelming. One student, the son of a Frenchman whose name was Columbus Bonfils, managed to sign up. Being financially destitute, I became desperate. I searched for a government job with no success. Finally, one of the authors of my letters of introduction contacted a teacher in the city who had a large school for boys and girls that needed an administrator. I contacted Mr. A.R. Plumley, and after an interview with him and his wife, Ms. Plumley, I secured the position. Mr. Plumley put me in charge of the boys' department, made up of eighteen or twenty pupils, to which I added my own student, Master Bonfils.[33]

My "Select Classical Seminary" had twenty pupils who studied a range of classical subjects. We pursued Latin and Greek languages, English Grammar, Geography, History, Mathematics, Rhetoric, Moral Philosophy, and several religious subjects.[34] My pupils were among the elites of Washington City, including the sons of Senator Henry Clay, U.S. Attorney General William Wirt, and other prominent men.[35]

Chapter Three – A Switch of Careers from Academics to Law

I T WAS NOT LONG BEFORE MY SCHOLARLY pursuits led one of my pupils' parents to enlist me for another purpose. In September 1827, Attorney-General Wirt encouraged me to join his law office as a student to read for the bar.[36]

Figure 5: U.S. Attorney-General William Wirt (Library of Congress)

It was not necessary to attend law school at that time to become a member of the bar – a certain amount of law office practice would do.

I became acquainted with the law-students and lawyers of Washington, attended sessions of courts and Congress, and became a member of the Blackstone Club of law students and attorneys, at one time serving as its president.[37]

It was not long before my natural inclinations in this arena drew me to the world of politics. What grabbed me was the case of Gilbert Horton.

Gilbert Horton was a free black citizen of New York who worked aboard a ship named *The Macedonian*. In the summer of 1826, the ship docked in Norfolk, Virginia. On July 22, Horton came to Washington on business, but was arrested and jailed on the suspicion of being a fugitive slave.[38] He was to be sold at auction to pay the costs of jailing him, as provided by District of Columbia law.

A short while later, John Owen, owner of a paper mill in Croton Falls, New York, received a package that had been wrapped in an August 1 edition of the *National Intelligencer*. Looking casually over the Washington newspaper, a notice caught his eye:

> "*Was committed to the jail of Washington County, District of Columbia, on the 22nd of July last, a runaway negro man by the name of Gilbert Horton. He is five feet high, stout made, large full eyes, and a scar on his left arm near the elbow; had on when committed a tarpaulin hat, linen shirt, blue cloth jacket and trousers; says that he was born free in the State of New York near Peekskill. The owner or owners of the above-described negro man, if any, are requested to come and take him away, or he will be sold for his jail fees and other expenses, as the law directs.*"[39]

Owen knew Horton, and knew that he was indeed a free man.

Owen brought the matter to the attention of William Jay, the son of John Jay, one of the signers of the Declaration of Independence, co-author of *The Federalist Papers*, and the first Chief Justice of the U.S. Supreme Court.[40] Together with the aid of New York Governor DeWitt Clinton, Owen and William Jay wrote a letter to President John Quincy Adams demanding Horton's release. They succeeded.[41]

The case stirred a controversy that had already been brewing in the District of Columbia concerning the odious presence of slavery and slave markets there. There were already calls for several years to abolish slavery in the District. A U.S. Representative from New York, prompted by the Horton case, submitted a resolution to Congress to determine whether District laws authorized "the imprisonment of any man of color and his sale as an unclaimed slave" to cover jail costs, which had been applied against Horton.[42]

Southern legislators were infuriated by the resolution. They suggested that it had been introduced solely to generate controversy over a District law that was identical to the laws of many states. The law was hotly debated and was finally referred to the Congressional committees governing the District of Columbia. Those committees upheld the legality of the law. In 1828, as this controversy roiled Congress, I jumped into the fray and assisted a group in drawing up a petition to Congress to abolish slavery and the slave trade in the District of Columbia.[43]

My impression of the members of Congress at this time was one of profound disappointment. Their indifference to appearances and the needs of the people was astonishing! On the floor of the House, one Representative would stretch out on a sofa trying to sleep; a group would be engaged in conversation; others would write letters or read newspapers.[44] I was not inspired to become one of them.

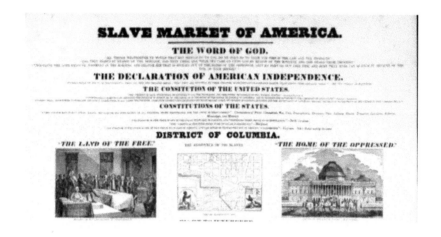

Figure 6: Part of a DC anti-slavery broadside issued during 1835-1836 petition campaign (Library of Congress)

Presently, in December 1829, I attended court to be examined for the bar of the District of Columbia. I was examined in the United States Circuit Court for the District of Columbia, which served as the District's highest local court, by none other than the illustrious Chief Judge William Cranch. After asking me a few questions, the Chief felt that I should study law for another year. I begged him to reconsider, as I had already made arrangements to go to the Western country to practice law. He accepted my plea and had me sworn in. [45]

Figure 7: Chief Judge William Cranch, circa 1844-1860 (PD)

Once I was admitted, I left Washington for Cincinnati, Ohio in
March 1830. I passed the Ohio Bar in June of that year and
commenced upon my legal career.[46]

Chapter Four – The Difficult Births of My Family Life and Legal Practice

———

HAVING LEASED AN OFFICE AND upon hanging out my shingle, which proclaimed that "SALMON P. CHASE, ESQUIRE, ATTORNEY AT LAW" worked therein, I began to suffer the queasy feelings that most young lawyers experience of having nothing to do and no one to administer to in my office. One does not hang a sign on one's window advertising a "SALE" on wills and trusts, nor place an advertisement in the newspaper announcing "Buy One Deed and Get Another One Free," as one might do when hawking one's wares. No, a lawyer must wait patiently until a potential client walks into the office with a particular type of problem that presents an opportunity for legal resolution that he can offer and receive payment for undertaking.

I did those things that most new young lawyers do, of course, to get my name mentioned around town and to attract the attention of an appropriate clientele. I published my business card as an advertisement in the *Cincinnati Daily Gazette* and waited at my desk for a reaction.

There was none.[47]

Early on, clients were few and far-between. One of my first clients, in fact, paid me a fee of a silver half-dollar on a Tuesday that he borrowed back on the following Wednesday, never to repay it![48]

In 1832, after an attempted law partnership with two other attorneys failed, I formed a new partnership with Daniel T. Caswell. The association proved to be very profitable for me because Caswell was the solicitor for the local branch of the Bank of the United States. My partnership entitled me to an equal share of the branch's legal business. The bank was the largest one in Cincinnati.[49]

Having thus adequately secured my financial affairs, I embarked on projects that would garner a measure of public attention to myself. I made frequent visits to the courthouse to watch cases, walk through the halls, and greet the many lawyers who stood with their clients outside courtrooms, waiting for their cases to be called to the bench. This was not an easy task for me, because I am a naturally shy fellow and I have somewhat of a speech impediment.[50] Fortunately for me, lawyers are a very talkative lot, and engaging in such conversations at the courthouse helped me beat back the frequent depressions of spirit that happen upon me from inaction.

I took the moot court classes offered by Cincinnati College to improve my public speaking.[51] Relying upon the letters of introduction that William Wirt had written to prominent lawyers in the city on my behalf, I was able to dine with men such as Daniel Caswell (my new law partner) and Joseph Benham.[52] I also made the acquaintance of Nicholas Longworth, the richest man in Cincinnati, whose acquaintance opened doors for me.[53]

By 1837, I had successfully handled some legal matters, paid some of my outstanding debts, and amassed a small savings that I proceeded to invest. I'm afraid to say, however, that much of that was lost in the nationwide financial panic of that year.

I spent some of my free time founding a lyceum in the city for the dissemination of useful knowledge to the public.[54] I prepared lectures for delivery at the lyceum. One subject in particular, a series of lectures on the life of Lord Brougham, ended up being printed as an article in the *North American Review* of January 1832 and was very favorably received.[55]

One major project that I embarked upon at the outset was a compilation of the Statutes of Ohio, which up until 1833 had been gathered into four volumes but had not been updated. The four volumes of statute laws that had been adopted by the Legislature of the State of Ohio were arranged only chronologically and were not at all indexed or annotated. There were also three volumes of enactments from the Legislatures of the Northwest Territories that had been promulgated between 1788 and 1833. There were also some thirty-one volumes of general statutes and local statutes from around the state.[56]

I compiled these laws, arranged, and indexed them by subject-matter in a rational way, and included below each statute reports of court cases that related to it. This treatise, which came to be known as *"Chase's Statutes,"* proved to be a great help to the legal profession that was rapidly developing in the northwest of the country.[57] It was not a moneymaker for me, however; only 150 copies were sold. [58]

- $ $ $ -

- $ -

Of the many projects in which I engaged at this time, the one that gave me the most trouble was my relationship with the opposite sex.

I certainly made an effort to attract young ladies to me. I could recite poetry and have always been fluent in French. The entertainment of young ladies and gentlemen of Cincinnati centered at that time in hotel and boarding-house parlors, where conversations covered many interesting topics. I flirted with many of the *doyennes* of the city – the daughters of William Wirt, Daniel Webster's niece Emeline, Nicholas Longworth's daughter Catherine. Alas, they were not as drawn to me as I was to them.[59]

As luck would have it, Eros nabbed me in a strange locale. At the hotel where I was boarding at that time, a family moved in there by the name of Garniss. John P. Garniss, the head of the household, was a local industrialist. He was a rather gruff and boorish social climber, and I took an instant dislike to him. Mrs. Amelia Garniss, his wife, was much kinder. Their daughter Catherine, whom they called "Kitty," was a somewhat affected and shallow girl with little real delicacy or refinement of character, it seemed to me.[60]

The family and I found ourselves thrown together socially many a time because of the proximity of our living arrangements. While I never warmed to Mr. Garniss, I came to appreciate Kitty more and more. She was well-versed in religion and literature, and was somewhat flirtatious with me. It was not long before, in March of 1834, we were married.[61]

Figure 8: Chase and his first wife, Catherine Garniss Chase, circa 1834

In November 1835, Kitty gave birth to a daughter, whom after a heated argument between Mrs. Garniss and me we decided to name Catherine Jane. The birth was normal, but Kitty felt somewhat sick afterward. She recovered, however.

Shortly after, I had the good fortune to be retained as counsel for the Lafayette Bank of Cincinnati, to represent it in important meetings in Philadelphia. This entailed my being in that city for some time, and upon discussing it with Kitty she favored my going as good for my legal reputation.[62]

I hurried home after my work was concluded, but on my way back to Cincinnati, I received a note in Wheeling, Virginia that Kitty's condition had worsened and she had died. I was overcome with grief and guilt for leaving her side to tend to business.[63]

My mother-in-law took upon herself the care of my baby daughter. We quarreled a good deal, but my sister Helen arrived from New Hampshire in 1837 to assist, and to act as a go-between my mother-in-law and me. She and I soon moved out of the Garniss's house to a residence of our own, close enough for them to dote on their granddaughter yet separate enough for us to stand one another. [64]

- $ $ $ -

- $ -

After a few years passed, a young woman caught my romantic eye once again. It was Eliza Ann Smith, the eighteen-year-old daughter of a middle-class property-owning family in Cincinnati. We married in September of 1839.[65]

The following January, scarlet fever struck the city of Cincinnati. Little Catherine Jane became violently ill and died in the home of the Garnisses. At the same time, we found that Eliza was two months pregnant. Joy and sadness arrived in my life together!

In August 1840, Eliza gave birth to a baby girl, whom we named Catherine Jane in her late stepdaughter's honor. We called her "Kate." That fall, another daughter was born, whom we named Elizabeth. But she died after three months.

In 1843, another daughter, whom we also named Elizabeth, was born.[66] She lived only one year, and died in July 1844.[67] Eliza had contracted tuberculosis during the pregnancy, and three years later, she too died.[68]

Some months later, I married yet again to Sarah Belle Dunlop Ludlow, the daughter of one of Cincinnati's leading abolitionists. In 1847, our daughter Janette Ralston, whom we called "Nettie," was born.[69] Sarah, too, died in 1852.

Among the many births and deaths of my wives and daughters, I was left by 1852 to be a widower three times over, with two surviving daughters. Kate and Nettie were to be great comforts and supports for the rest of my life.

Chapter Five – James Birney and Matilda's Case

―――

A MIDST THIS SOMEWHAT ROCKY START, the great legal issues of the day began to make their way to my doorstep.

Cincinnati, the first large city in a free state on the Ohio that stood across the river from the slave state of Kentucky, was a crossing point for fugitive slaves anxious to escape from bondage to freedom. Article 4, section 2 of the U.S. Constitution and the federal Fugitive Slave Act of 1793 required the return of escaped slaves found in free states to their masters in slave states. Many localities in the North weakened this law by acting as sanctuaries and passing local ordinances that required jury trials for the recapture of escaped slaves. Often, the juries would nullify the law and free the slaves. [70] The citizens of Cincinnati, however, mostly supported the slave-holders' privilege to capture runaway slaves crossing over the Ohio.

James G. Birney, a southern lawyer and slave-holder, emancipated his slaves in 1833 and thereafter dedicated his life to abolition of that "peculiar institution." In 1836, he established the *Philanthropist* in Cincinnati, an anti-slavery newspaper.

Figure 9: James G. Birney, Abolitionist—(PD)

The city, however, was rife with vehement pro-slavery sentiment. It wasn't long before a mob invaded the newspaper's offices in the middle of the night and damaged its printing presses. A large public "meeting" was held thereafter, presided over by the mayor, to determine whether the city would tolerate "the publication or distribution of abolition papers in Cincinnati."[71] The mob demanded Birney's abandonment of the newspaper as the only way to avoid violence.

Anti-slavery societies in the city offered the pro-slavers a public discussion of the issue. The latter, however, wanted nothing to do with it. One evening later, rioters again entered and destroyed the offices of the *Philanthropist*, scattered type all over the streets, and threw the printing presses into the river. Thereafter, the rioters attacked Negro homes in the city.[72]

I had nothing to do with these events, but they affected me deeply. My New England upbringing and religious training went against the grain of many Cincinnatians, who had come to southern Ohio from Virginia, had close family ties to central Kentucky, and had lived with slavery as a routine part of their lives. They were inured to the horrors of a slave society – the chain gangs of Negroes, both young and old; the whippings, often on the public street; the forcefulness of bounty hunters seizing fugitive slaves wherever found and hauling them off to the auction block; the auction block itself. To my way of thinking, there was nothing to be gained from enslaving one to work when paying a living wage would do just as well.

My higher education, like Mr. Birney's, differentiated me from the backwoodsmen and laborers coming from the South who had learned little or nothing of our Declaration of Independence or our Constitution, both of which fostered equality among men. I resolved, at that point in my life, to do all that I could to aid the abolitionist cause.In March 1837, Mr. Birney gave me that chance – he called upon me to represent a captured fugitive slave in court.[73]

- $ $ $ -

- $ -

Matilda was a mixed-race housekeeper who worked in the Birney mansion. She had been hired when Mrs. Birney was recovering from a difficult childbirth and needed assistance around the house.[74] The Birneys were under the impression that Matilda was a free colored woman. However, after having served the Birneys for several months, Matilda revealed that she was in fact a runaway slave.[75]

Matilda had been owned in Virginia by Larkin Lawrence, a citizen of Missouri. She may have been Lawrence's daughter, and he permitted her to pass as such in public and in private. On a trip down the Ohio River to Missouri, the boat on which Lawrence and Matilda were traveling docked at Cincinnati. While the boat was docked, Matilda left it and sought refuge in the city with the family of a black barber. He sheltered her until the boat left to continue its trip to St. Louis. [76]

Lawrence made no effort to find Matilda after she escaped. Fatefully, however, he mentioned her disappearance to local slave catchers in Cincinnati before he left on the boat for St. Louis.

Once it seemed safe to do so, Matilda secretly sought employment and was hired by the Birneys.[77] Sometime after Matilda confessed her situation to them, Mr. and Mrs. Birney decided to wait and see if anyone would notice. After a while they made her a permanent servant in their household. Unbeknownst to them, however, Matilda was being watched by the slavecatchers to whom Lawrence had spoken.[78]

On March 10, 1837, a constable appeared at the Birney's door with a warrant for Matilda's arrest, sworn out by one John M. Riley, a well-known fugitive slave bounty-hunter in the city, purportedly acting as an agent of Larkin Lawrence. Matilda was seized, arrested, and led off to jail.[79]

That very afternoon, Mr. Birney showed up at my office.

"Mr. Birney!" I stood from my desk, extending my hand in greeting to one of the few prospective clients who ventured through my door at that time. "What a pleasure to see you! What brings you to my office that I can do for you?"

"Good afternoon, Mr. Chase," said Birney, with a downcast look on his face that one rarely saw on him. "I need your legal help. A terrible event happened at my home this morning. My servant, Matilda, a mulatto, was arrested in front of my home as a fugitive slave and taken off to jail!"

"Matilda?" I replied with surprise. "I met her the last time I was at your home. I had no idea that she was a mulatto. She seemed to me to be a white woman."

"Her white slave-owner is her father," Birney said. "That dastardly slave-catcher, Riley, swore out a warrant as agent for her father and the constable took her away. Not only is Matilda in serious trouble, but so am I, possibly, for harboring a fugitive slave."

I knew Birney to be a fine lawyer, educated at the College of New Jersey.[80] "That is true, Mr. Birney, and I know that I do not have to remind you of the provisions of the federal Fugitive Slave Act of 1793," I said. "You could be fined very heavily."

"You may call me James," Birney told me politely. "May I call you Salmon?"

"I prefer 'Sam,'" I replied, with a bit of my stammer in my voice. "Salmon" was a mouthful for most people and always generated a smirk or joke from my listeners because of its relationship to a species of fish. I had always much preferred the more familiar "Sam" to my given name.

"Very well, then," James replied. "Sam, we must act quickly. Riley may whisk Matilda away and have her sold into slavery at any moment. These slave-catchers are rogues and have no respect for due process. They usually claim to be the agents of the real owners but usually have no connection to them at all. Riley may very likely secure her release from jail by hook or by crook and have her transported and sold this very day, without ever going before a judge!

"I have no doubt, Sam," he continued, resting his hand on my shoulder," that you are the man to help me right this wrong and clear my name."

"I am honored, James, and I will gladly take the case," I said to him. "In a way, we are fortunate that Matilda is in jail. Riley cannot just act without seeking a judicial writ or bribing the constable. We have no cause of action under the Fugitive Slave Act, but we can file a writ of *habeas corpus* to get her out of jail and taken before a federal judge to seek her release."

"I agree, Sam, that is the only way," said James. "I only wish that we had some evidence of Matilda's free-born status to present to the court."

"Well, James," I attempted meekly to inject at least a little levity to raise his spirits, "when one doesn't have the facts, one pounds the law. When one doesn't have the facts or the law, one pounds the table."

"We may owe the Court for the price of broken furniture," James muttered morosely.

- $ $ $ -

- $ -

Figure 10: Judge David K. Este, Sr., circa 1862

Judge David Kirkpatrick Este, Sr., was at this time the President Judge of the Ninth Judicial Circuit of Ohio.[81] The same day that James Birney walked into my office, I filed a petition for a writ of *habeas corpus* with the Judge on behalf of Matilda. Judge Este set the trial date for the following day. I had no time to prepare. James and I worked furiously that afternoon and evening before the hearing to frame the case for Matilda.[82]

We sat at my conference room table late into the night, discussing the facts and precedents that we had found in the law books and composing legal arguments.

"We have to find precedent regarding the condition of slaves in transit, because Matilda was transported by her master from the slave state of Virginia to the free state of Ohio," I said to James by the light of the oil lamp. "It seems to me that the key to this case is Lawrence's voluntary transfer of Matilda from a slave state to a free state, which would counteract the charge that she *escaped on her own* from her master in the slave state and *fled on her own* to a free state."

"That does seem to be the most promising avenue," James replied.

"In reading a Massachusetts case just now," I went on, "I happened upon the English case of *Somerset v. Stewart*, in the Court of King's Bench in 1772.[83] It posits the exact situation that we have now.

"The facts are," I continued," that James Somerset, an African slave to Charles Stewart in Virginia, was brought over to England by his master. Once in England, Somerset quit his master's service. Stewart had Somerset forcibly detained on Captain Knowles' vessel, the *Ann and Mary*, without Somerset's consent. Mr. Stewart planned to have Somerset transported on that ship to Jamaica for sale in the slave market there. A writ of *habeas corpus* was applied for by English friends of Somerset before the Chief Justice, Lord Mansfield. Captain Knowles brought Somerset before the Court.

"As to Somerset's having refused service to Stewart and having been detained on Captain Knowles' ship for sale into slavery in Jamaica, Lord Mansfield ruled that such an 'act of dominion' over a person must be supported by some 'positive law' of the country where it is being used. Mansfield decided that the act is 'so odious that nothing can be suffered to support it, but positive law.' As there is no such 'positive law' in England,' Mansfield held, Somerset must be discharged."[84]

"That ruling was in 1772?" James asked me. "That predates the Declaration of Independence. Then it is good law here!"

"There was a similar case in New Jersey," said I, "wherein the Supreme Court there held that in a free state, a fugitive slave or white apprentice cannot under the Fugitive Slave Act be deprived of his liberty without being granted procedural rights, including a trial by jury as provided by the New Jersey constitution."[85]

"So," James interjected, "slavery, being contrary to natural right, can exist wherever it does only by virtue of positive law, and such a law has no force and effect beyond the borders of the state which has enacted it! Therefore, that law vanishes when the master and slave find themselves together in a territory where no such law exists!"

"But," I said, pulling James back on his reins, "Ohio is bound by Article 4 of the U.S. Constitution to return fugitive slaves to their rightful owners."

"Hmm."

We sat silently together for some time and pondered this dilemma.

"Wait!" I remarked presently. "I've already said it! Matilda is not a fugitive! Lawrence voluntarily brought Matilda from Virginia to Ohio; she did not *escape* from her master at all! As she was in the free state of Ohio, no positive law existed to bind her to her master. She was a free woman here when the boat she was in docked in Cincinnati!"

"Well, that will have to do at this point," James said. "It's worth a try, but it depends on the notion that a slave-holder cannot transport his slaves out of his native slave state without losing his power to own his slaves. We both know that slave-holders transport their slaves across state lines all the time, and they don't expect that to happen when they do it. You're arguing, effectively, that the Fugitive Slave Act is unconstitutional, and yet it is right there in Article 4."

"We'll just have to see what kind of judge Judge Estes is, I guess," I said.

- $ $ $ -

- $ -

"So, the Fugitive Slave Act is unconstitutional; is that your argument, Mr. Chase?" A dubious Judge Este stroked his beard and looked sideways out the courtroom window.

We'd just finished our closing argument before a gallery packed with spectators – Cincinnatians love court hearings. I was present with Matilda, James, and my partner, Sam Eels. Three prosecutors faced us for the jailors.[86]

"No, Your Honor, in light of Article 4 of the Constitution I cannot argue that," I admitted somewhat hesitantly. "I contend that neither the Fugitive Slave Act nor Article 4 apply here because Matilda is not a fugitive. Lawrence voluntarily brought Matilda into Ohio, a free state. There is no positive law in Ohio that sanctions slavery or permits persons to be seized without due process of law. Therefore, once in Ohio at her former master's behest, she was no longer a slave, but a free woman in a territory that does not know of slavery at all. Not being a slave or a fugitive at that moment, she was not subject to the Fugitive Slave Act and could not be seized."

"If, however, Your Honor finds that the Fugitive Slave Act applies," I continued, "then you must recognize that there is no act of Congress that authorizes the issuing of a state process in the name of the state, in any case whatever under that Act. Then there is a failure of due process that is guaranteed by the Constitution of the State of Ohio, and in the absence of constitutional process in the Act, Matilda must be discharged."

It was a weak finish, but I had to rest on the only straw that I had left.

Matilda, seated next to me, sat quietly in her chair, staring at her hands in her lap. She was slight of figure, plainly dressed in her best cotton dress with a kerchief wrapped around her head. Her fists were clenched together at the wrists, as if a pair of manacles were holding them together. I am sure that she read Judge Este's skeptical face as well as I could.

Judge Este looked down at his desk for a few moments, then looked up. "Counsellor, I cannot accept your argument. The Fugitive Slave Act of 1793, by its own words, forbids a slave from escaping 'into *any other part of* the said States or Territory.' It makes no distinction as to whether the fugitive slave escapes into a *different* state or the *same* state. And so, it does not rely on whether the state into which the slave escapes recognizes slavery as a matter of its own 'positive law' or not. I think that the Fugitive Slave Act is clearly constitutional and the supreme law of the land, and the prisoner, therefore, is not discharged.

"Matilda is remanded to Mr. Riley's custody as agent for Mr. Lawrence. The petition is dismissed." The Judge banged his gavel and called for the next case. Riley and two of his accomplices seized the terrified Matilda right out of her chair at our counsel table and hustled her, screaming and crying, out of the crowded courtroom. [87]

- $ $ $ -

- $ -

I later learned that Matilda never made it back to Larkin Lawrence. Instead, Riley conveyed her immediately to a waiting ship on the pier to be transported to St. Louis. She disappeared entirely; she was most likely sold in the slave market without Lawrence ever learning of it.[88]

James and I were both devastated by the loss. She had done nothing, absolutely nothing, to warrant Riley grabbing her out of her chair, hauling her off like a common criminal and spiriting her away to imprisonment, hard labor, and regular beatings and rapes. The utter imbecility of this way of life weighed on my soul. No day could go by without some manifestation of it – a public whipping, the passing of a chain gang guarded by a ruffian with a rifle, the shouts of brokers at the slave auction block showing off their wares and dickering over prices. I learned much from the experience that would serve me in later cases of the same kind, of which there would be many.

And Matilda's case served me well when James called upon me to defend him in the suit for violating the Ohio state law against harboring a fugitive slave. This was the most imbecilic aspect of the whole system: not only were Negroes enslaved, but whites were enslaved as well by the system's entrapment for shielding a Negro, regardless of whether he or she was a fugitive slave or not.

I made the same argument for James, before a jury and the same judge, that Matilda was not a fugitive and James, therefore, was not guilty of harboring one. Although the jury ruled against James and Judge Este fined him $50 on the verdict, the Ohio Supreme Court reversed the judgment on appeal, finding that Birney could not have known whether Matilda was a slave or free person of color when he had hired her. In that circumstance, and most certainly in the case of a wealthy white man with a reasonable excuse, the legal presumption favored freedom.[89]

Chapter Six – On To the Senate

———

A FTER *MATILDA'S CASE*, MY REPUTATION as a dedicated abolitionist lawyer grew – for better *and* worse – throughout the Ohio Valley. I came to be known as the "attorney-general of runaway negroes."[90] Not that I liked the nickname, mind you. Representing the poor tends to reduce an attorney's fees. But here in Cincinnati, on the border between freedom and slavery, my legal business became brisk indeed.

Figure 11: U.S. Supreme Court Chief Justice Roger B. Taney, circa 1850 (PD)

My arguments in that case proved to be a model which was followed in similar cases throughout the Northern states that challenged the constitutionality of the Fugitive Slave Act.[91] They proved to be successful in some instances, but ran into opposition upon appeal to the U.S. Supreme Court, particularly under the pen of Chief Justice Roger B. Taney, a Maryland Southerner and slave-owner.[92]

My anti-slavery stances in court propelled me into the political limelight. By the 1840s, Stephen Birney and I were actively engaged in forming an abolitionist party that we called the "Liberty Party." [93] We later helped form the "Free-Soil Party," which was dedicated to preventing the extension of slavery into the unorganized territories of the United States that had been won from Mexico in the war (of which more later). At bottom, however, I still viewed myself as a Democrat because I believed in the ideals of Thomas Jefferson – that of a rural, agriculturally-based country rather than one of national planning and high tariffs imposed by a strong central government, as the Whigs preferred. I also believed in "hard money;" that is, money backed by gold or silver, referred to collectively as "specie." And, of course, it was vital to my career aspirations to be a Democrat because Cincinnati was solidly Democratic.[94]

My political position on slavery diverged from the view of hardline abolitionists, who believed that the institution was unconstitutional *per se* in all of the United States. I preferred the view that the Federal Government could ban slavery everywhere in which it had exclusive jurisdiction – the territories and the District of Columbia. But in the states, it could only be removed by state law. This view pleased neither Northern abolitionists nor the Southern Slave Power. To the North, it allowed for the *preservation* of slavery where the political will to ban it did not exist; to the South, it denied slaveholders their property rights in violation of the Due Process Clause of the Fifth Amendment.[95]

The Free-Soil Party approved of my views. In 1848, the Ohio State Legislature fell into their hands. I lobbied them for two things: to repeal the "Black Codes," laws that discriminated against free blacks; and to appoint me as Ohio's next United States Senator. I won both demands.

I served as a Free-Soiler in the Senate from 1849 to 1855. I joined with Democrats who fought against passage of the Kansas-Nebraska Act (more on that later).[96] Once the Republican Party was formed, I was nominated by it for Governor of Ohio and served in that capacity from 1855 to 1860.[97]

My political star continued to ascend. I was spoken of among Republicans as a worthy candidate for President of the United States, and my name was placed in the running for that Party's nomination in the election of 1860. But after three grueling ballots at the Republican Convention, Abraham Lincoln was chosen. As a consolation, the Ohio Republicans in the Legislature appointed me as their U.S. Senator once again, commencing in 1861. I accepted the position and prepared to resume my old post in Washington.

Others, however, had different plans for me.

PART TWO
LINCOLN

Chapter Seven – The National Crisis Evolves

———

A S MY LIFE AND CAREER FLOURISHED, the young republic that I loved and served withered.

The Founders, when they wrote the Constitution, were clearly of a mind that slavery would soon become extinct. *Somerset's Case*, the 1772 English decision that I had relied upon heavily in *Matilda's Case*, hastened the demise of slavery throughout the British Empire. It officially ended there in 1833 upon the passage of an act of Parliament.[98] *Somerset's Case* was widely reported in the Thirteen Colonies and, I think, may have played a role in prompting the South to revolt against the Empire. The Founders were clearly comfortable enough with the then-prevailing presumption of slavery's ultimate demise to insert into the Constitution a grant to Congress of authority to ban the importation of slaves after the year 1808.[99]

By 1840, several states had already banned slavery *and* the slave trade – all of New England and Pennsylvania by shortly after the American Revolution; all of the states carved by the Northwest Ordinance out of that Territory; and New York, gradually, between 1799 and 1827. The Missouri Compromise of 1820 banned slavery in all states that were to be formed out of the Louisiana Purchase except Missouri, Louisiana, and Arkansas.[100]

But the Founders could never have foreseen Eli Whitney's invention of the cotton gin. The cotton gin's mechanization of the laborious process of hand-brushing seeds out of white cotton fibers impelled plantations in the South to burgeon in size and enlarge their slave populations.[101]

Figure 12: Stephen Duncan, Slave Owner

With slave importation into the United States now banned and British warships plying the oceans hunting down illegal traders, the American South developed its own "peculiar institution" of domestic slave breeding and marketing. The slave trade soon came to be referred to by Northern abolitionist orators as the "Slave Power," a dark force of businessmen and bounty-hunters who supplied bodies to the plantation owners for work in the cotton fields. Moguls of the Slave Power gained ignominious reputations, like banker Stephen Duncan of Mississippi, one of the largest slave-owners in the United States, who ran fifteen cotton and sugar plantations that shackled 2,200 slaves.[102]

Our war with Mexico settled the issue of Texas annexation, which concluded in 1848 with the Treaty of Guadelupe-Hidalgo between the United States and Mexico. In addition to Texas, that treaty incorporated the vast territories that made up the northernmost Mexican states of Santa Fe de Nuevo Mexico and Alta California into the United States, gigantic tracts of unsettled land that doubled the size of our country.

The United States and its territories now stretched from the Atlantic Ocean to the Pacific. Slavery had already been abolished in these Mexican lands, but the potential for vast new fields of cotton, sugar and rice was not lost on the Slave Power. The compromises of the past that had been based on the belief that slavery was doomed to extinction were swept aside by this new economic force. It pressed in favor of the enormous world-wide profits to be made from enlarging cotton production on the backs of slaves. Its promoters infiltrated the halls of the U.S. Congress and agitated to repeal the Missouri Compromise, eager to spread their nefarious industry throughout the newly-annexed land.

- $ $ $ -

- $ -

The politician who most strongly advocated for the interests of the Slave Power was Stephen Arnold Douglas. A Democrat, Douglas was first a Representative, then a Senator, from the state of Illinois.

Figure 13: U.S. Senator Stephen A. Douglas of Illinois

Douglas did not profess to be pro-slavery. Rather, he professed to the role of an honest broker, negotiating compromises between the North and the South. I and others, however, saw Douglas's machinations as the Slave Power's *sub rosa* effort to punch holes in the Missouri Compromise so it could expand its "peculiar institution" to as much of the western territories as the nation could tolerate.

Douglas entered the Senate in 1847, just as the Mexican-American War was getting underway. Once we secured Alta California and Santa Fe de Nuevo Mexico from our neighbor, abolitionists formed a counter-movement to ban slavery in any new state that was to be

GREENBACK 57

formed out of the new lands (Texas, having been an independent republic at its annexation, already had slaves and was not part of this plan). The "Wilmot Proviso," as the bill that was devised to accomplish this aim was called in honor of its author, Representative David Wilmot of Pennsylvania, was vehemently opposed by Southern congressmen. The Proviso passed the House but was defeated in the Senate. Douglas, while still a Representative, voted against the Proviso in concert with the Southerners, even though he represented the free Northern state of Illinois.

Now the Southerners went on the offensive about what to do with slavery in the new territories. Senator Henry Clay of Kentucky, author of the Missouri Compromise of 1820, offered a new deal in 1850. California was the first population to explode in size, and sent a proposed state constitution to Washington for approval that banned slavery in the new state. First, Clay offered the abolitionists the admission of California as a free state. Second, he offered to cede the northern and western territorial claims of Texas along eastern bank of the upper Rio Grande River to the Federal government in return for debt relief for the new state of Texas. Third, Clay proposed the creation of the Utah and New Mexico territories out of the Mexican and Texan cessions, saying nothing about slavery there but leaving it to the imagination that New Mexico would become slave and Utah free. Last, Clay offered a ban on the importation and sale of slaves in the District of Columbia, to be offset nonetheless by a stronger fugitive slave law.

Opponents reviled Clay's compromise in both houses of Congress. Advancing age was catching up with Clay, and in December 1851, as the debate raged, he took a leave of absence from the Senate and later resigned. He died six months later.

Stephen Douglas, together with President Fillmore and Senator Daniel Webster, took up the cudgel for Clay's compromise. The package was divided into separate portions and passed through the House and Senate piece-by-piece.

Next, the pro-slavery faction in Congress took on the issue of the admission of new states that were forming in the unorganized remainder of the Louisiana Purchase territory. In 1854, Douglas proposed organizing part of it into the Kansas and Nebraska territories, presumably to facilitate the development of a transcontinental railroad. Instead of adhering to the Missouri Compromise, Douglas proposed that the citizens of each new state would determine its free-or-slave status by popular vote, a concept that he called "popular sovereignty."

We abolitionists knew that this ruse guaranteed the advance of slavery into territories where it had been banned by the Missouri Compromise. Although Kansas was north of the Missouri Compromise line, it was likely to be settled by Southerners. They would be encouraged to move into Nebraska too, opening both territories up to slavery by their popular votes. The Missouri Compromise would be extinguished.

Stephen Douglas's "popular sovereignty" sham fulfilled the North's worst expectations, and in the bloodiest of ways. It provoked the undoing of the Union.

Chapter Eight – Kansas Bleeds

———

THERE TURNED OUT TO BE NO "POPULAR SOVEREIGNTY" in Kansas – instead, there was total, brutal, inhumane civil war.

Kansas rested just north of Latitude 36° 30' North, the boundary running east to west between slave and free lands under the old Missouri Compromise. Slavery was permitted in new states that were formed south of that line, but not north of it. But the slave-state of Missouri *was* just north of the line, and Kansas was directly west of Missouri. Inevitably, settlers from Missouri entered Kansas and brought their slaves with them.

The settlers of Kansas split between "free-soilers" – those who opposed the introduction of slavery – and pro-slavery men. The two formed rival provisional governments – free-soilers established their capital first in Lawrence, then in Topeka; pro-slavers established their capital in Lecompton. Two separate state constitutions were proposed and drafted. Two separate provisional state legislatures were seated.

Soon, war broke out between armed thugs from each side. The territory came to be known in Eastern newspapers as "Bleeding Kansas." The feud lasted from 1854, when Kansas's admission to the Union was proposed and passed by the U.S. House of Representatives, until January 1861, when enough Southern senators from seceding states had left the U.S. Congress to enable the remaining Northerners to pass the bill making Kansas a free state.

During the "Bleeding Kansas" conflict, President Pierce, and President Buchanan after him, supported the pro-slavery men of

Kansas and supplied them with arms and ammunition. New England abolitionists, led by the Brooklyn preacher Henry Ward Beecher, exhorted Northerners to move to Kansas and fight for a free state.

Figure 14: Henry Ward Beecher, circa 1860 (Library of Congress – PD)

The most famous of these settlers was John Brown of Ohio, whose band murdered proslavery citizens of the Kansas prairie in what became known as the "Pottawatomie Massacre." Brown committed more violent acts against the Slave Power until, in 1859, he was captured by Colonel Robert E. Lee of the U.S. Army and hanged at Harper's Ferry, Virginia for instigating and arming a slave revolt there.

Figure 15: "Tragic Prelude," Mural in the Kansas State Capitol

While our country bled on the Kansas prairie, Abraham Lincoln of Illinois began his campaign for the Presidency.

Chapter Nine – The Ascent of Lincoln

M R. LINCOLN WAS A TALL, LANKY MAN with an easy Western manner, a high-pitched voice, and a prodigious cache of backwoods humor. Originally a member of the Whig Party, Lincoln served eight years in the Illinois House of Representatives, then spent two years serving his Illinois district in the U.S. House of Representatives. After his single Congressional term ended in 1849, he spent the next decade practicing in Springfield as a railroad lawyer.

Figure 16: Abraham Lincoln, circa 1858 (PD)

Like many others, Lincoln was angered by the Kansas-Nebraska Act and the Kansas civil war. The Whig Party met its demise over that conflict, and the Republican Party was born out of it. Republicans did not object to slavery's continued existence in the South, but were determined to ban it from the western territories.

In 1858, Lincoln, now a Republican, challenged Douglas for the latter's re-appointment to his seat as U.S. Senator from Illinois. The state legislature would make the choice, and to coax legislators one way or the other, the two candidates agreed to a series of seven debates in front of their constituents across the state. The debates were attended by thousands of spectators.

In the third debate in Jonesboro that September, Douglas made clear his position on slavery in the territories and on race in general:

> *Mr. Lincoln likens that bond of the Federal Constitution, joining Free and Slave States together, to a house divided against itself, and says that it is contrary to the law of God, and cannot stand…. Now, I say to you, my fellow-citizens, that in my opinion, the signers of the Declaration had no reference to the negro whatever, when they declared all men to be created equal. They desired to express by that phrase white men, men of European birth and European descent, and had no reference either to the negro, the savage Indians, the Fiji, the Malay, or any other inferior and degraded race, when they spoke of the equality of men. One great evidence that such was their understanding, is to be found in the fact that at that time every one of the thirteen colonies was a slaveholding colony, every signer of the Declaration represented a slaveholding constituency, and we know that not one of them emancipated his slaves, much less offered citizenship to them, when they signed the Declaration; and yet, if they intended to declare that the negro was the equal of the white man, and entitled by divine right to an equality*

with him, they were bound, as honest men, that day and hour to have put their negroes on an equality with themselves. ...

My friends, I am in favor of preserving this Government as our fathers made it. It does not follow by any means that because a negro is not your equal or mine, that hence he must necessarily be a slave. On the contrary, it does follow that we ought to extend to the negro every right, every privilege, every immunity, which he is capable of enjoying, consistent with the good of society. When you ask me what these rights are, what their nature and extent is, I tell you that is a question which each State of this Union must decide for itself...[103]

Douglas's statement recited quite concisely the view of race and slavery in America as the Slave Power of that day held it. In the debate at Jonesboro, Lincoln refuted it:

[Judge Douglas asks], "Why can't we let [slavery] stand as our fathers placed it?" That is the exact difficulty between us. I say that Judge Douglas and his friends have changed it from the position in which our fathers originally placed it. I say, in the way our fathers originally left the slavery question, the institution was in the course of ultimate extinction, and the public mind rested in the belief that it was in the course of ultimate extinction. I say, when this Government was first established, it was the policy of its founders to prohibit the spread of slavery into the new Territories of the United States, where it had not existed. But Judge Douglas and his friends have broken up that policy, and placed it upon a new basis, by which it is to become national and perpetual. All I have asked or desired

anywhere is that it should be placed back again upon the
basis that the fathers of our Government originally placed it
upon. I have no doubt that it would become extinct, for all
time to come, if we but readopted the policy of the fathers,
by restricting it to the limits it has already covered, —
restricting it from the new Territories....[104]

That was precisely the way that we Abolitionists saw the future of America unfolding. The Declaration of Independence meant what it said when it proclaimed that "all men are created equal." The Northwest Ordinance of 1787 banned slavery in the Northwest Territory because the Confederation Congress viewed slavery to be dying out. The Founders likewise foresaw in 1776, by holding that "all *men* are created equal," that slavery was ending throughout the land.

Although in the end the Illinois Legislature reappointed Douglas for another Senate term over his rival, Lincoln's effort was not in vain. His debates with Douglas propelled him to the top of the list of potential Presidential candidates for the election of 1860, a list I was on as well.

- $ $ $ -

- $ -

One of those who had heard of Lincoln by this time was James A. Briggs, a Cincinnati lawyer and good friend of mine, and a fellow campaigner during our road trip around Ohio in 1848 to stump for the Free-Soil Party's presidential candidate, Martin Van Buren (sadly, an unsuccessful effort).[105] In the late 1850s, Briggs was working with Abolitionist Pastor Henry Ward Beecher's Plymouth Church in the City of Brooklyn. Briggs was engaged by the Church to promote a lecture series that it was sponsoring. Briggs telegrammed Lincoln, asking him to give a speech in the series "on any subject you please" and offering to pay Lincoln $200 for it. Lincoln accepted, on the condition that it could be a "political speech."[106] The Church managers of the lecture series, however, balked at the expensive fee and on the subject matter of giving a "political speech" in a House of God.[107]

The New York Young Men's Central Republican Union, however, was very interested in hearing Lincoln speak. They offered to move the lecture series from Brooklyn to Manhattan and to include other political speakers as well. The series was moved to Cooper Union and set for the winter of 1860, at the start of what was shaping up to be a watershed Presidential election year.

The Young Men's Republican Union arranged not only for an appearance by Lincoln, but also Francis Preston Blair, a confidant of President Andrew Jackson and former owner of the *Congressional Globe*. They also sought out Cassius M. Clay, the famous Kentucky abolitionist. Lincoln would give the third and last speech in the lecture series. He was delighted to have this chance for Northeasterners to see and hear him, as they were still relatively unaware of his growing popularity in the West.

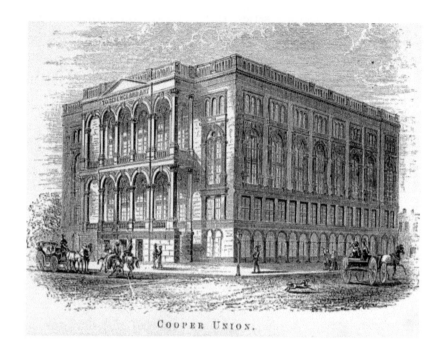

COOPER UNION.

Figure 17: Cooper Union, New York City (PD)

- $ $ $ -

- $ -

I did not attend Lincoln's speech, which was held on February 27, 1860. I had declined an invitation from William Cullen Bryant the year before to speak in New York, which proved to be a missed opportunity for my presidential ambitions. Instead, the spotlight turned to Lincoln.

I received a letter from Briggs after the speech while I was home in Cincinnati. He reported on it to me in the most glowing of terms. [108]

"A large audience attended the speech in the Great Hall of Cooper Union," he wrote. "Horace Greeley was there, and William Cullen Bryant introduced Lincoln to the audience. That could have been you only one year before, Sam," Briggs tweaked me reproachfully.

"Lincoln is tall, gangly, and, I must admit, somewhat ugly in appearance," Briggs wrote me. "His new suit did not fit him very well."

Figure 18: Abraham Lincoln on February 27, 1860, on the day of his Cooper Union Speech (PD)

"He has a very shrill voice, almost painful to the ear. I could see eyes rolling in the audience. But once Abe got going, we were all positively spellbound!"

From what I read of the newspaper account of the speech, Lincoln began his hour-and-a-half presentation by recalling the interpretation that Senator Douglas had given during the Jonesboro debate to the Founders' view of slavery, as Douglas saw it, when they wrote the Constitution. Lincoln recounted how, out of 65 men who were authorized by their respective states to attend the Constitutional Convention, 10 never showed up. Of the 55 who made it, 16 did not stick around long enough to sign the great document; only 39 of them did. These men, Lincoln therefore concluded, were the country's true "Founders."[109]

The government that these 39 men framed, said Lincoln, was set forth in a Constitution that was made up "of the original, framed in 1787, ... and 12 subsequently framed amendments, the first 10 of which were framed in 1789."[110] These men, as Senator Douglas had put it during the Jonesboro debate, understood slavery "just as well, and even better, than we do now."[111] But what, in fact, *was* their understanding, Lincoln asked? He saw it this way:

> It is this: Does the proper division of local from federal authority, or anything in the Constitution, forbid our Federal Government to control as to slavery in our Federal territories? Upon this, Senator Douglas holds the affirmative, and Republicans the negative. ...Let us now inquire whether the "39," or any of them, ever acted upon this question; and if they did, how they acted upon it – how they expressed that "better understanding."[112]

Lincoln examined the voting records of the "39" in the Confederation Congress and the First Congress under the Constitution on the prohibition of slavery in the Northwest Territories. He said that when the subject first came up in the Confederation Congress in 1784, three years before the Constitution was adopted, four of the "39" were members and three of them voted in favor of the ban. In 1787, when the Northwest Ordinance containing that same ban was adopted by that same Congress, two more of the "39" were then members and voted in favor of the Ordinance's prohibition of slavery. In 1789, Lincoln said, a bill to enforce the Northwest Ordinance under the new Constitution came before the first U.S. Congress, in which sixteen of the "39" sat, and it passed unanimously. George Washington, then President and another one of the "39," signed the bill into law.[113]

Figure 19: Lincoln Speaking at Cooper Union

Lincoln continued that when in 1804 Congress considered a bill to organize that part of the newly-purchased Louisiana Territory that would become the State of Louisiana, slavery was already established there and Congress did not attempt to prohibit it. But Congress regulated it, said Lincoln, by banning the importation of slaves into the territory from outside the United States and limiting their domestic importation to those slaves who were brought in by their owners. Two more of the "39" were present in that Congress, which passed the bill unanimously. Again, in 1820, two more of the "39" participated in the vote on the Missouri Compromise – one voted to allow slavery but the other voted to prohibit it.[114]

Thus, Lincoln told the audience, 23 out of the 39 "Founders" – the majority of them – had voting records demonstrating "that, in their understanding, the proper division of local and Federal authority did not forbid the government from prohibiting slavery in the Territories." What is more, Lincoln informed the audience, of the remaining sixteen Founders, "three were the most noted anti-slavery men of that day – Benjamin Franklin, Alexander Hamilton and Gouverneur Morris." Only one of the sixteen, John Rutledge of South Carolina, "was known to be a pro-slavery man," said Lincoln. [115]

Lincoln thus trounced the view of Senator Douglas on the Founder's view of the extension of slavery to the territories. But he did much more; he also refuted the *Dred Scott* case—the Supreme Court decision written by Chief Justice Roger B. Taney three years before Lincoln appeared at Cooper Union. That infernal screed overturned the Missouri Compromise. Of the Founders and of the men who made up the First Congress under the Constitution, Lincoln proclaimed, "I defy any man to show that any one of them ever, in his whole life, declared that in his understanding, any proper division of local from Federal authority, or any part of the Constitution, forbade the Federal Government to control ... slavery in the Federal Territories."[116]

Lincoln spoke further; he appealed to the South to come to its senses, and to Republicans for calm and moderation. He nevertheless condemned the South's position.[117]

By well before this time in his talk, Briggs informed me in his letter, the whole audience in the Great Hall of the Cooper Union was convinced.

The morning after, Horace Greeley gushed in the *New York Daily Tribune*:

> *Mr. Lincoln's speech excited frequent and irrepressible applause. His occasional repetition of his text never failed to provoke a burst of cheers and audible smiles. The completeness with which Popular Sovereignty and its progenitor were used up has rarely, if ever, been equaled. At the conclusion of his speech Mr. Lincoln received the congratulations of a large number of his friends and the friends of Republicanism.*[118]

By mid-May, the Cooper Union speech had catapulted Lincoln to the head of the list of candidates for the Republican nomination for President. On May 8, at the Republican National Convention in the Chicago "Wigwam," Lincoln beat Seward, myself and five others for the nomination on the third ballot. I must confess that I did not try very hard to win it.[119]

Figure 20: Chicago Wigwam, Site of 1860 Republican National Convention (PD)

The election that November was calamitous. The Democrats split into two conventions, one Northern and one Southern. The Northerners chose Stephen Douglas; the Southerners chose John C. Breckinridge. Former members of the now-defunct Whig and Know-Nothing Parties formed a new party, the Constitutional Union Party, and nominated John Bell of Tennessee for President. Lincoln and Douglas competed for Northern votes while Breckinridge and Bell competed for Southern ones.

On Tuesday, November 6, 1860, the four-way race ended with Lincoln receiving nearly 40 percent of the largest voter turnout up to that time, amounting to over 81 percent of the total electorate. He carried the North, the West, California, and Oregon. No ballots for Lincoln were cast in ten Southern slave states. In the end, Lincoln received 180 electoral votes out of a total of 303, a clear and decisive majority.[120]

Abraham Lincoln was inaugurated as the sixteenth President of the United States in Washington, D.C. on March 4, 1861. By that time, seven Southern states had seceded and four more would follow.[121]

Chapter Ten – A Call to Duty

———

OF ALL THE CALAMITIES THAT SLAVERY begat, none was more disastrous to me than the prospect of disunion.

In South Carolina, electors for President were chosen by the State Legislature rather than by a popular vote of citizens. After the national vote, the Legislature met on the same day as all other states to select its electors, as the Constitution requires. But it remained in session after the choice was made to see whether electors for Lincoln would predominate across the country, and when that became evident, they passed resolutions to convene a secession convention. [122]

The convention met on December 17, 1860 in Columbia, the capital of South Carolina, for the purpose of "restoring" the state's independent "sovereignty."[123] Moving then to Charleston, the convention on December 20 passed an ordinance of secession which declared that the "Union now subsisting between South Carolina and other States under the name of *The United States of America* is hereby dissolved."[124] Five neighboring Southern states followed shortly thereafter, intent on disuniting peaceably if possible, but by war if necessary.

I stood squarely at that time for maintaining the Union, and said so. "If the executive power of the nation were in my hands," I wrote a friend in New Orleans, "I should know what to do. I would maintain the Union, support the Constitution, and enforce the laws."[125] But, I wrote my friend, "I would not shut my eyes to the fact, manifest to everybody, that it is from the slavery question that our chief dangers arise, and I would direct whatever influence I might possess to an adjustment of it – not by any new compromise, for new compromises can only breed new dangers – but by honest provision for the honest fulfillment of all constitutional obligations connected with it."[126]

I would have left the institution of slavery in the slave states alone as an internal state matter that is not the Federal Government's business. But the secessionists, by provoking disunion, were defeating their own purpose of extending slavery into the Federal Territories because they were foregoing their ability to accomplish it. Was there any way other than by brutal war by which they could extend slavery into territories that they no longer controlled?

- $ $ $ -

- $ -

Shortly after the election, I received a telegram from Mr. Lincoln inviting me to a conference with him in Springfield.[127] I left Columbus immediately by train, and arrived in the capital of Illinois on January 3, 1861. When I arrived at my hotel, I found the lobby crammed with politicians contending with one another for federal offices and other sinecures from the President-elect.

No sooner had I arrived in my room and began unpacking my bags when there was a knock at my door. It was none other than President-elect Abraham Lincoln himself.

"Senator Chase?" Lincoln said with a smile, doffing his stovetop hat that had added nearly two extra feet to his towering frame, "I am so pleased to see you! Welcome to Springfield! I am sorry for the unannounced intrusion, but I have something to discuss with you of great importance. May I come in?"

"Why, of course ...Mr. President-elect," I replied, not quite sure if what I called him was politically correct.

"You may call me 'Abraham,' or 'Abe' if you prefer," he said, smiling again. "Everybody else does. I have heard that you are known to others as 'Sam.' Is it all right if I call you that?"

"Why, yes ... Abraham," I stammered. "Actually, I much prefer it."

"Wonderful!" Abe said. "May we sit down?" There was a small table at one end of the room, and we pulled two chairs up to it.

As we sat, Abe said, "You know, Sam, I have always felt grateful to you when, back in '58, you came to Illinois to help me out in my debate with Senator Douglas."

"Oh, yes!" I recalled. "I think, Abe, that as that series progressed across the state, more and more people warmed to your points. I think the reason why you are President-elect now is that you ably captured exactly what the common people believe are at stake."

"I agree with you that they did," Abe replied. "I have you to thank for your coaching and mooting of my arguments during our practice rounds."

"I was honored to do it, and I'm thrilled that it led to so much success in your career!" I said.

"And that brings me," Abe leaned forward, clasping his large hands around his raised right knee, "to my reason for asking you to come out here. I am doing with you what I would not venture to do with any other man in the country ..."

"*That* is an interesting *entrée*," I thought to myself. Lincoln is busying himself lately with filling his cabinet and other government positions. I have thought a great deal about becoming Secretary of State, although I know that Bill Seward covets that spot. What might Abe have in mind for me?

"... I've sent for you," Abe continued, "to ask you whether you will accept the appointment of Secretary of the Treasury."

I was stunned. Of all the many jobs that I've had in my life, I have never thought of myself as facile in any way with handling money. How could I manage handling the finances of the United States?

Before I could speak, however, Abe raised a hand and added, "I ask this, Sam, with the *caveat* that, in truth, I am not exactly prepared right now to offer the position to you."

Now I was puzzled. What type of "offer" is this?

At last, I spoke up. "Well, Abe, uh, that places me in an unpleasant position," I said. "I am not anxious to be offered an appointment, mind you," I stated in order to maintain the freedom to turn the President-elect down if I felt that the job did not suit me. "But," I added, "I could not easily reconcile myself to the acceptance of a subordinate one."

"Oh, I am aware of the talk of making you Secretary of State, Sam, and I'm sure you consider that position to be the right one for you. And it may indeed be, except that Mr. Seward is generally recognized to be the leader of the Republican Party, and I feel bound by politics to offer it to him first. In fact, he has already accepted it."

"I see," I replied, concealing my dejection at the news.

Sensing my displeasure, Lincoln jumped in to explain himself further to me. "My intent, however, was that if Seward were to decline the job, then I would have offered it to you, without qualification. That doesn't mean that I wanted Mr. Seward to decline, of course. I truly wanted him to accept it, and I'm glad to say that he has."

So, I now thought. Obviously, the conservatives in the Party are the ones who control Lincoln. They are anxious to compromise with the Southern secessionists and preserve the Union, which can only be accomplished by allowing slavery to invade the western territories by some Douglas-style Congressional artifice. I must be considered as too deep into the Abolitionist camp for those peoples' comfort. The Department of State is surely too policy-oriented to leave to one such as myself. Better to leave me to the numbers, I brooded dejectedly to myself.

On the other hand, I pondered, a bird in hand is worth two in the bush, as hunters say. I did not want to appear disinterested in the Treasury position, so as not to embarrass the President-elect and to keep my options open, come what may.

"Abe," I said, "I concur with you that Mr. Seward should be offered the job of Secretary of State, and that he is indeed the right man for the job. I have to say that at this moment, I am not yet prepared to declare my willingness to accept the Treasury position if it is offered to me. But if Mr. Seward has accepted the State position, then I have no qualms about Treasury being a subordinate position if I should decide to accept it in lieu of representing Ohio in the Senate."

Abe seemed to think for a moment. His political purpose for seeing me now having been done with, the President-elect exercised his prerogative to change the subject. He let go of his knee and shifted back in his seat in a more relaxed pose.

"All right, then," he said next. "Well! Let me ask you another question. What is your opinion of offering the Southerners an extension of the Missouri Compromise line through the territories, stopping at the California border, of course, in order to preserve the peace?"

"I could not agree with that at all, Abe," I replied. "I think the Republican Party platform is clear, that there is to be no extension of slavery into the territories at all. The Missouri Compromise line changed the understanding of the Founding Fathers that slavery was destined for total extinction, as you yourself said during your debates with Senator Douglas.

"'No extension' means *no extension*," I emphasized. "Slavery does not exist in New Mexico now, which is just as the Mexicans had left it. It would be tantamount to an international crime, I think, to force it upon them now that we have succeeded to ruling that territory."

Abe again paused, then turned to pick up his hat from the table. "Well, Sam," he said, "I'm very glad that we've had this conversation. I think I understand your way of thinking much better now. I have made no decision at all as to whether to compromise with the Southerners or not, but I stand by the Republican Party platform and I think you succinctly state it.

He stood. "Let's talk again soon, shall we? I have many things to think over, and I would greatly appreciate your wise counsel whilst I have you here in Springfield."

"I would be honored, Abe," I replied. We shook hands warmly. Abraham Lincoln placed his hat on his head and strode out of the room.

Chapter Eleven – A Last-Ditch Effort to Avoid War

———

D URING THE REMAINING MONTHS after the election and before the President-elect was to be inaugurated on March 4, 1861, the "lame-duck" outgoing Congress held several conferences and made several attempts to arrive at a compromise between the free states and the slave states that remained in the Union. All Congressional attempts failed.

Once I had returned to Columbus, the Legislature of the Commonwealth of Virginia, uncertain as to whether it would secede, passed resolutions declaring "that unless the unhappy controversy which now divides the States of the Confederacy shall be satisfactorily adjusted, a permanent dissolution of the Union is inevitable."[128] Although Virginia was still in the Union at that time, the Legislature offered "an invitation ... to all such States, whether slaveholding or non-slaveholding, as are willing to unite with Virginia in an earnest effort to adjust the present unhappy controversies, in the spirit in which the Constitution was originally formed, and consistently with its principles, so as to afford to the people of the slaveholding States adequate guarantees for the security of their rights ... ."[129]

The wording "in which the Constitution was originally formed" was a dead giveaway that the "invitation" was being extended by the pro-slavery side of that Legislature as a cover to justify their view, consistent with Taney's *Dred Scott* decision, that withholding slavery from the territories would be a denial of their property rights under the Due Process Clause of the Fifth Amendment. Hardcore

Abolitionists denied the constitutionality of slavery everywhere, whilst Republicans like myself more moderately accepted slavery where it was already established by or before the Missouri Compromise, but not in the Federal territories where that Compromise had excluded it, nor in the Federally-governed District of Columbia.

The Virginia resolutions proposed that the invited states "appoint commissioners to meet on the 4th of February next, in the city of Washington, similar commissioners appointed by Virginia, to consider and if practicable agree upon some suitable adjustment." [130] Virginia named five "commissioners" for the Commonwealth: former President John Tyler, William C. Rives (longtime Congressman and Ambassador to France), John W. Brockenbrough (a federal judge), George W. Summers (a Congressman and judge), and James A. Seddon (a former Congressman).[131]

Newly-elected Governor William Dennison, Jr. of Ohio, who succeeded me in that office when I was appointed to the U.S. Senate, accepted Virginia's invitation and appointed me to be a delegate to the "Peace Conference" on behalf of Ohio, together with Thomas Ewing (first Secretary of the Interior during the Taylor/Fillmore administration), William S. Groesbeck (former U.S. Representative from Ohio), John C. Wright (former Ohio Supreme Court Justice), Reuben Hitchcock (a railroad executive), and Franklin T. Backus (a lawyer).

Seven slave states and fourteen free states sent delegations to the conference.[132] It met on February 4 at the Willard Hotel in Washington, D.C. It presented a stellar cast of 131 delegates – former cabinet members, ex-governors, former senators, former representatives, twelve state supreme court justices, and one former president.[133]

Those of us on the anti-slavery side learned that day that the seven already-seceded states (Texas had joined the original six a short time later) were meeting simultaneously in Montgomery, Alabama to form a new republic among themselves, to be known as the "Confederate States of America." The "Confederates" were lobbying Virginia heavily to join them. It became painfully obvious to us that this "conference" was just a ploy on Virginia's part to obtain without secession that which the Confederates were now offering the Commonwealth in return for joining them.

Figure 21: The Willard Hotel, Washington, D.C. (PD)

A committee consisting of one member for each state was formed to draft a proposal for the conference to consider. After three weeks, the thirteen members of the committee produced a proposed constitutional amendment consisting of seven articles:

1. **To revive the Missouri Compromise line through the territories, dividing them between a slaveholding south and a non-slaveholding north;**
2. **To prohibit new acquisitions of territory without the assent of a majority of Senators from each of the slaveholding and non-slaveholding states;**
3. **To prohibit Congress from interfering with slavery in any state where it existed; or in the District of Columbia without the consent of Maryland and that of the slaveowners of the District; or in any territory where it was established by territorial law; and to prohibit Congress from interfering with the slave trade between the states;**
4. **To prohibit any construction of the Constitution against the Fugitive Slave Law;**
5. **To prohibit the foreign slave trade;**
6. **To prohibit any amendment to the Constitution against slavery without the concurrence of all the states; and**
7. **To provide compensation from the United States to any slaveowner whose fugitive slaves were liberated from him by mob violence.**[134]

To those of us from the free states, this proposal was unconscionable. It was nothing less than a total capitulation to the Slave Power to do whatever it wanted in the territories. On February 6, as the conference pondered this proposal, I delivered a speech to condemn it, and I offered a counterproposal.

I suggested that the proposed constitutional amendment was premature, and that the conference should be adjourned for two months so that Lincoln could be peacefully inaugurated.[135] This conference, I said, cannot substitute its judgment of what the People want to have done. The election of Lincoln was not a fluke, I said. "I believe, and the belief amounts to absolute conviction, that the election must be regarded as a triumph of principles cherished in the hearts of the people of the Free States."[136] They do not want extension of slavery into the territories.

I urged the slaveholding states to accept the principle that I had argued as early as in *Matilda's Case*. It was that the free states, and Lincoln as well, seek to restrict slavery within state limits; "*not* war upon Slavery within those limits, but fixed opposition to its extension beyond them."[137] The free states have always preserved the slave states' rights.[138] Fears in the South of aggression from the North to destroy slavery in the slave states are groundless, I implored them.

Clearly, this position did not meet everything that the Slave Power wanted. It was no longer enough for slavery to remain secure in the existing slave states; the Slave Power craved *economic expansion*, and its new-found greed could not be satisfied by maintaining what it already had.

As for the odious fugitive slave bounty-hunting that had developed in the country that slave-owners sought to preserve, I proposed the following compromise – that fugitive slaves found in the territories and states where slavery is prohibited not be returned to their masters, but instead that the masters be compensated from the U.S. Treasury for their loss. As for the Fugitive Slave Clause stipulated in the Constitution on which the South relied to make the North return runaways, I said, the people of the Free States "who believe that slaveholding is wrong, cannot and will not aid in the reclamation, and the stipulation becomes, therefore, a dead letter."

[139] "Instead of a judgment for rendition," I explained, "let there be a judgement for compensation, determined by the true value of the services, and let the same judgment assure freedom to the fugitive. The cost to the National Treasury would be as nothing in comparison with the evil of discord and strife. All parties would be gainers."[140]

This, too, was unacceptable to the slave states. The Slave Power included not only the slave-owners within its economic sphere, but the bounty-hunters too. They would not tolerate their lucrative industry being abolished by my "compensation" scheme.

The proposed amendment, I argued to the conference, would never be ratified by Congress or the states. If this were simply a means to defeat the conference's original purpose to arrive at a compromise, then I could understand it. But, I said, "[a]s a measure of pacification, I do not understand it. There is, in my judgment, no peace in it."[141]

I ended my argument with this warning to the Southern delegates:

> *Gentlemen, Mr. Lincoln will be inaugurated on the 4th of March. He will take an oath to protect and defend the Constitution of the United States – of the whole – of all the United States. That oath will bind him to take care that the laws be faithfully executed throughout the United States. Will Secession absolve him from that oath? Will it diminish, by one jot or tittle, its awful obligation? Will attempted revolution do more than Secession? And if not, and the oath and the obligation remain, and the President does his duty and undertakes to enforce the laws, and Secession or revolution resists, what then? War! Civil war!...[L]et us not*

rush headlong into that unfathomable gulf. Let us not tempt this unutterable woe. [142]

On that note, I sat.

The conference put the proposed amendment to a state-by-state vote, and it was approved by 11 state delegations to 9, with the Ohio and Virginia delegations in favor. [143] Only one other Ohio delegate and I opposed it. [144]

As I expected, the proposed amendment was thereupon presented to the Senate, which rejected it out of hand. The House of Representatives never even considered it. [145]

Chapter Twelve – I Become Secretary of the Treasury

———

W ITH HOPES FOR RECONCILIATION WITH the slave states dashed, I remained in Washington through early March to be inaugurated into the Senate. On March 4, 1861, after President Lincon's inauguration concluded, I proceeded to the Senate Chamber, where I was sworn in, and took my seat there.

A couple of days later, I excused myself from the Senate chamber and proceeded to my assigned office in the U.S. Capitol. I sat down at my empty desk, surrounded by empty bookshelves. I had not yet hired any staff. No one came to visit me. I felt bored. I got up and returned to the Senate chamber.

Figure 22: Senator Lyman Trumbull of Illinois

As I entered, Senator Lyman Trumbull, a good friend of mine, strode up the aisle to shake my hand. "Congratulations, Sam!" he said.

Puzzled, I said, "for what?"

"Why, President Lincoln just nominated you for Treasury Secretary and we've consented to it unanimously! You're in the Cabinet now!"

"I am?" I exclaimed. Strange – neither the President nor anyone from the White House had informed me that he had acted on our discussion and had finally chosen me, much less that he had forwarded my nomination to the Senate and instantly won approval.

"Er ... excuse me, Lyman, I must go to the White House immediately to speak to the President."

"You'd better hurry, Sam," Lyman replied with a laugh. "I hear Abe is up to his ears in allegators already!"

- $ $ $ -

- $ -

After a quick ride down Pennsylvania Avenue in a hansom cab, I climbed the steps to the White House door, strode up the stairway, and entered the President's office. The President and his two personal secretaries, John Hay and John Nicolay, were arranging books in the wall shelves and rearranging furniture that ex-President Buchanan had left behind.

"Well, Sam!" The President stepped off a stepstool by the shelves (why he needed one given his height, I couldn't tell). He grinned widely as he extended his hand to me. "Congratulations! I trust you've heard by now."

"Yes, Mr. President," I replied, gripping his hand somewhat tentatively. "I was not in the Senate Chamber when it happened. I must tell you, and I'm truly sorry to do so, but ...er ... I am disinclined to accept the position, sir."

"Oh?" said Abe, the unusually intense creases lining his face shifting deeply downward from happiness to troubled surprise.

"When you spoke to me about it a couple of months ago, I told you that I wanted no appointment and could not easily reconcile myself to the acceptance of a subordinate position if the State Department were to go to Mr. Seward. Secretary of the Treasury is a subordinate job for a man of my talents, which behooves me to stay in the Senate, representing Ohio."

Having said that, I was immediately unhappy with the way it sounded. Mr. Lincoln frowned.

"Well!" he replied dourly. "This is very embarrassing, I must say! After we talked, I left under the distinct impression that you would nevertheless think about it. Is that the conclusion that you reached after giving it some thought?"

"Well, Abe, ... I mean, Mr. President," I haltingly responded, "to tell you the truth, I did not have the opportunity to give it a great deal of thought because of all the activity that I found myself engaged in at the time, what with the peace conference and the appointment to the Senate and all."

Abe's frown remained planted on his face. "Well, I think you *should* think about it, Sam! Secretary of the Treasury is *not* a 'subordinate position,' as you call it. Not only that, I *need* a man of your brains and caliber in the Cabinet.

"This country is in great peril! You came very close to convincing the Southerners not to leave the Union at the peace conference, and that skill at compromise and settlement is something that I will sorely need!"

I was very worried about my blundering response. The President of the United States is not a man to be trifled with, regardless of whether a homespun backwoodsman like Abe looks the part or not. Arousing his ire and embarrassment was something I knew could have a disastrous effect on my future political prospects. If I wanted to run against him for President one day, he would be able to hold my rejection against me and my reputation would suffer greatly. On the other hand, accepting this position now would potentially marry me to the mistakes that he would be bound to make in the next four years.

Of course, it was *also* true that he genuinely *was* in a fix. The South held him to be personally responsible for all their differences with the North, as if he singlehandedly caused them all. He most certainly needed moderate statesmen of high repute, like myself, to help him deal with the irate secessionists.

"I see, Mr. President. Perhaps ... I have not thought this through carefully enough. I have no desire whatsoever to let you or the country down. May I think it over tonight and advise you of my decision tomorrow?"

"I can give you until tomorrow, Sam," Abe said pointedly to me as he turned to the bookshelf behind him. "I sympathize with your disappointment in not getting the State job, but the needs of the time can't always be tailored to meet one's desires."

"I fully understand, Mr. President," I responded. "With your permission, I bid you good-day until tomorrow."

"Good-day, Sam," Abe said, turning his back on me to climb the stepstool.

- $ $ $ -

- $ -

I returned to the Senate, quite shaken by what I'd just been through. Once there, I ran into Lyman Trumbull again. He was sitting at his little desk in the chamber, reading a newspaper. He looked up at me and removed his spectacles.

"Sam, you look like you just saw a ghost."

"I went to see Lincoln, Lyman. I told him that I didn't want the Treasury job."

"You turned Lincoln down?"

"I told him that I'd think about it."

"Sam!" Lyman barked, "Abe is counting on you to be in his Cabinet! He needs you there! What the hell is wrong with Treasury?"

"It's not the State Department, for one. Even worse, I'm not a numbers man, Lyman."

"Sam, that's just the point! If we go to war, have you any idea how financially unprepared for that this country is?"

"Yes."

"Well, it's going to take a very smart lawyer to convince the New York and London banks to back the Union if we go to war with the South!" Lyman's voice was echoing across the half-empty chamber. "Their relationships with the cotton brokers of New Orleans are extraordinarily close. The Boston milliners are panicking at the thought of losing the cotton trade to England! One of the biggest battlefields in this war is going to be on Wall Street, Sam! Abe wants a good lawyer on that battlefield with him."

"You damn well better not turn down that job," Lyman warned me as he replaced his spectacles on his nose and turned back to his paper.

That evening, I ate dinner at the Willard Hotel alone. I was not so much depressed now at being given a job that I didn't want as I was ashamed of my behavior toward the President of the United States. How could I have been so stupid as to think only of my hurt feelings when the country was in such danger and needed a man of my capabilities?

I decided then and there to resign from the Senate and accept the President's offer.

I wrote to Ohio's Governor Denison my letter of resignation. After asking him to forward my resignation to the State General Assembly, I stated:

> It would be far more consonant with my wishes to remain at the post to which the people of Ohio, through the General Assembly, saw fit to call me. Deeply indebted to their generosity for repeated marks of confidence, and for the profoundly indulgent consideration with which my endeavors to promote their interests have ever been regarded by them, it is impossible for me to prefer any other service to theirs.

> But the President has thought fit to call me to another sphere of duty, more laborious, more arduous, and fuller far of perplexing responsibilities. I sought to avoid it, and would now gladly decline it if I might. I find it impossible to do

so, however, without seeming to shrink from cares and labors for the common good, which cannot be honorably shunned. I shall accept, therefore, these new duties, greatly distrusting my own abilities, but humbly invoking divine aid and guidance.[146]

Chapter Thirteen – The Yawning Trench

O N THURSDAY, MARCH 7, 1861, AFTER a brief swearing-in ceremony at the White House, I strolled down Pennsylvania Avenue to the building next door – the U.S. Treasury Building. It is the most imposing edifice in the City of Washington, even more so than the U.S. Capitol itself, although the latter would overshadow it soon with a massive new dome.

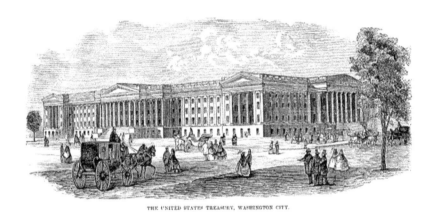

THE UNITED STATES TREASURY, WASHINGTON CITY.

Figure 23: The U.S. Treasury Building, circa 1860 (PD)

Upon entering my new office on the third floor of the building, I was greeted by George R. Harrington, who had served for the past twelve years as the Chief Clerk of my predecessor Secretaries. I had already heard great things about his superlative capabilities as an administrator and had every intention of retaining him in the position.[147]

"Good morning, Mr. Secretary!" Harrington greeted me warmly, shaking my hand. "Welcome to the Department of the Treasury!"

"Good morning, Mr. Harrington," I replied. "I am very glad to meet you. I want you to know that I have heard of your excellent abilities in your position and I respectfully request that you continue in them. With a raise in pay, of course."

Harrington's face brightened. "Why, thank you Mr. Secretary! I certainly did not expect *this* felicitous a greeting from you! I am most grateful for your trust in me."

"My pleasure, sir," I replied. I had to admit, I was warming to this job. I did not expect my new office to be as grand as it turned out to be. There is a large private office and an even larger adjoining reception room. The windows look out upon a view of the broad expanse of Pennsylvania Avenue that ends at the hill on which sits the U.S. Capitol. Murals representing "Treasury" and "Justice" adorn the office's immense ceiling, with Treasury seals in each of the four corners.[148]

Figure 24: Secretary's Office, Treasury Department, circa 1860 (PD)
[149]

I surmised that the best way to start off with my new chief employee was to get right down to business.

"So, Mr. Harrington. Tell me. What do I need to know to do this job?"

He laughed. "Oh, a great deal, sir! I too know your reputation, sir, and I'm sure that you will master it in no time. Shall I start with the current state of federal finances?"

"That sounds like a good place to start." We sat in two elaborate chairs facing a magnificent fireplace in the middle of a long wall of the office. A warm fire was already burning there.

"It is best understood by hearing where the U.S. stands in the sale of government stocks and bonds. At certain times, Congress authorizes the Treasury to sell government bonds and government stocks to raise funds by borrowing from the public. Government stocks are sold as they are in the private market, with each stock having a 'par value,' but paying interest instead of dividends. Treasury sales of stocks yield purchase offers greater than par value and can be sold and resold in the private markets. Government bonds are auctioned off at a discount from their face-value and pay periodic interest as well. Their face-values are paid to the holder on the maturity dates of the bonds.

"Our most recent auction was last December. Congress authorized the Treasury to issue ten million dollars of one-year Treasury notes paying interest at the best rate attainable. That turned out to be 12 percent per annum.[150] That is a high rate, but it comes as no surprise in view of the political situation. The notes were sold at a discount from face-value, and the difference between face-value and what we get for each note represents the bond purchaser's return on the loan.

"We auctioned off five million dollars' worth of the authorized ten million dollars in one-year notes on December 28, 1860. The discounts that purchasers offered us, however, were quite high – we collected only between twelve and thirty-six percent of the notes' face-values. That came to an income for the Treasury of only about a half a million dollars."[151]

"Twelve to thirty-six percent!" I exclaimed. "That's outrageous!"

Mr. Harrington winced. "Needless to say, Mr. Secretary, the 'full faith and credit' of the United States Government is at a very, very low ebb these days."

"And what became of the rest of the ten million dollars that were authorized?"

"We disposed of that in January of this year," Harrington replied. "For only eleven percent of face-value.[152]

"We sent a letter to the Chairman of the House Committee on Ways and Means this past February," Harrington continued. "We informed the Committee that the liabilities of the Government that were to fall due on March 4 were about ten million dollars, and that the revenues of the Treasury Department were wholly inadequate to meet them. We told the Committee that eight million dollars would have to be borrowed."[153]

I gasped. "I take it that the fact that you are here today means that you are getting paid, and that some way around this problem was found!?"

"Yes," said Harrington. "In February, Congress authorized a loan of $25 million in United States stocks, payable between ten and twenty years out and bearing six percent annual interest. We received about $14.5 million for them, accepting discounts that left us at between 75 and 96 percent of face-value."[154]

"What became of our good fortune," I interjected, "when President Jackson announced in 1834 that the Government had paid off its Public Debt in full in that year? Not only for the expenditures incurred during the Revolution, but the War of 1812 as well?"

"Ah, yes," said Harrington. "Subsequent government revenue after that year was largely surplus, so in 1836 Congress authorized it to be allocated to the states in proportion to their Congressional representation and deposited in their treasuries. It was to be returned to the Treasury as provided by law, but to date Congress has not asked for it back. It has assisted the states greatly in bolstering their own borrowing power, of course, but at the Federal Government's expense."[155]

"Undoubtedly, the Senators and Congressmen from those states consider that arrangement to be just fine," I sniffed.

"Yes, they do, Mr. Secretary. And now, with one third of the country in rebellion and forming its own nation, the Union has lost an immense financial resource in the form of tariffs at Southern ports, investments from Southern plantations, and various forms of internal revenue, not to mention the services of numerous Southern banks.

"We can expect, moreover, that the Southerners will nevertheless insist that the Treasury pay the interest due on the U.S. Treasury bonds and stocks that they hold, in gold and silver. Their future investments in bonds and stocks, however, will go to the Confederate Treasury, not to us."

My mind was swimming in these facts and figures. I had absolutely no idea what to make of them or how to handle them. This was far beyond my mere ability to reconcile my charge account with the local grocer.

"Er, tell me, Mr. Harrington, how much clear, unencumbered authority do I have to float loans at this moment?"

He thought for a moment, then walked over to my desk, opened a drawer, and pulled out a pad and pencil. "Well, sir, we have the Act of June 22, 1860, the Act of February 8, 1861, and the Act of March 2, 1861. The first Act allows us to issue $21 million of United States stocks at six percent per annum. Your first predecessor in the Buchanan Administration, Secretary Cobb, negotiated away

$7,022,000 of that. So that leaves us with $13,978,000 in remaining authority." He wrote that figure on the first page of the pad.

"The second Act," he continued, "allows us to issue $25 million of United States stocks at six percent, and your second predecessor in the previous Administration, Secretary Dix, negotiated away $8,006,000 of that, leaving us with $16,994,000 in remaining authority." He wrote that figure on the page, immediately below the first one.

"Finally, the third Act allows us to issue $10 million of United States stocks at six percent, and no negotiations have occurred on that to date. So, we have $10 million more there." He wrote that figure below the other two.

Harrington added the figures up. "That leaves us with $40,972,000 in unobligated borrowing authority to use."[156]

"And we already must pay $10 million in bills coming due now with only about $2 million currently in the Treasury, leaving us with $8 million left to borrow. And this is just to stand still!"

I looked up at Harrington's impassive face, the face of one who has been dealing with this crisis for a long time and is no longer awed by it, as I am.

"Mr. Harrington? Let me dwell on this a bit and call you in again at another time. We have a great deal to do, and we must do it in a hurry."

"Of course, Mr. Secretary," Harrington said. He stood, bowed, and walked out the door without another word.

- $ $ $ -

- $ -

For the next several days, I arrived at my office early in the morning and sat there alone for most of the day. Mr. Harrington would venture in after I settled myself and brought in the morning newspapers, files, and memoranda for the day's meetings. As he was about to exit, he would ask me if I wanted a cup of coffee, and I always responded, "Black."

I would carefully read the memoranda, look at the files, and peruse the newspapers. Washington City, now filled up with politicians, lobbyists, office-seekers, lawyers, and reporters of all political persuasions after a quiet winter, was desperately missing one key contingent – soldiers.

The United States Army at this time was under the command of General Winfield Scott, the venerable hero of the Mexican-American War. Aging, obese, and ill, Scott remained loyal to the Union despite his Virginia roots. He implored the outgoing Buchanan Administration to reinforce Washington and certain forts along the coastline of the seceded states – Fort Sumter in the harbor of Charleston, South Carolina; and Fort Pickens in the harbor of Pensacola, Florida. Other Union forts in the South were abandoned to the Confederates.

Figure 25: Winfield Scott, Commanding General of the U.S. Army in 1861 (PD)

Scott saw to it that President Lincoln was inaugurated peacefully in Washington on March 4, 1861. When the President-elect sent an emissary to General Scott beforehand to ascertain his loyalty to the Union and his willingness to preserve order at the inaugural events, Scott informed him:

> *I shall consider myself responsible for* [Lincoln's] *safety. If necessary, I shall plant cannon at both ends of Pennsylvania Avenue, and if any of the Maryland or Virginia gentlemen who have become so threatening and troublesome show their heads or even venture to raise a finger, I shall blow them to hell.*[157]

That was comforting.

Across the Potomac River, Virginians were mulling over the failure of the Peace Conference to reconcile their differences with the North over slavery. They decided somewhat treacherously to play off both opposing camps. When the Viriginia General Assembly passed its resolution convening the Peace Conference, it simultaneously called a state convention to consider whether Virginia should secede. Delegates were elected on February 4, 1861 and convened immediately in Richmond.

Two-thirds of the delegates favored staying in the Union, which was a comfort to those of us across the river, but the debate and rancor at the convention between Unionists and Secessionists was intense. The Confederate Congress sent three commissioners to the convention to lobby for Virginia to join them. They warned the delegates that the Republican Party, now in control of the United States government, intended "the ultimate extinction of slavery and the degradation of the Southern people."[158]

I spent most of those fraught early days in the Administration wracked by anxiety. I went through the motions of my daily work, but I was at a loss as to how to prepare the country for the war that was sure to come at any moment.

I continued holding the bond auctions, advertising an $8 million loan at six percent interest to be awarded on April 2. I felt certain that these stocks would sell at par, but in case they didn't, I set a floor for offers of 94 percent of par and declined all offers below that.[159] We raised $7,814,809.80, which was encouraging because the floor held despite many cantankerous remarks from bankers and brokers. [160]

On April 4, we floated two-year Treasury notes at six percent interest and raised another $4,901,000. The notes sold at par value.[161] This was a better result, but we were still dangerously short of meeting our mounting expenditures.

On April 12, the Confederates bombarded Fort Sumter. It fell into their hands the next day. On April 14, President Lincoln called a meeting of the Cabinet. We met at the White House throughout the night to draft a call for troops from the states remaining in the Union and to plan for the defense of Washington and the border states. We called for Congress to convene a special session on July 4 to appropriate funds for the war effort.[162] The coincidence of choosing that day for the special session with the anniversary of our Declaration of Independence was intentional.

On April 17, Virginia seceded from the Union and joined the Confederacy. North Carolina, Tennessee, and Arkansas followed soon after. Pro-Confederate mobs threatened Missouri and Kentucky, but those states did not secede. Mobs in Baltimore cut rail lines from the North, isolating Washington.[163] General Scott did what he could to recruit loyal militia companies for the city, but willing men and available munitions were in short supply.[164]

On April 22, I received word from the new customs collector that I had just appointed for the port of Baltimore. He informed me that his trip from his home in Western Maryland to his post at the Baltimore Harbor was interrupted by mobs shouting "Black Republican" and "Maryland traitor" at him, threatening to pull him off his train and lynch him, and warning him not to occupy his post. He gave up trying to do so.[165]

In late May, as Northern sentiment over the firing on Fort Sumter reached a fever pitch and troops were being mustered in those states, I raised another $8 million in an auction. On July 4, I raised another $2.5 million.[166] All told, we now had enough money in the Treasury to get the government through the special session of Congress.[167] That was all.

PART THREE
COOPER

———

Chapter Fourteen – Peter Cooper Becomes a Wealthy Industrialist

Figure 26: Peter Cooper, date unknown (PD)

AS I FOLLOWED MY CAREER PATH up to this stage, a gentleman was busy creating an industrial empire for himself in New York City.

Peter Cooper was an inventor almost from his birth in 1791. He had no formal education. All his prodigious knowledge of mechanics was self-taught.[168] From a small factory in Hempstead, Long Island, where he made machines for shearing off the rough surface, or "nap," of woolen cloth in order to create a smooth surface on the fabric,

[169] Peter made good money from the boom in textile manufacturing that arose in New York and New England during the War of 1812 as a result of the U.S. embargo on importing foreign materials.[170]He married Sarah Bedell of Hempstead in 1813, bought a home there, and patented numerous inventions, even including a self-rocking cradle for his first son that also played lullaby music.[171]

When the end of the War of 1812 decimated the fledgling American textile industry, including Cooper's business, he moved his family to New York City, which at the time was growing inexorably northward up Manhattan Island.[172] There he established a grocery store with his father-in-law, but shortly afterward acquired a failing glue factory at Fourth Avenue and Thirty-third Street for a small sum. Through tireless effort, he upgraded the factory's manufacturing process and acquired patents for his glue-making improvements. Cooper then developed a method for making isinglass (a collagenous substance from fish swim bladders that is used in the cooking of gelatins). Now firmly cemented in the lucrative glue-making and gelatin trade, Peter Cooper proceeded to become a wealthy man.[173]

Cooper grew even wealthier when he next entered the emerging business of railroading. He built a steam locomotive, the *Tom Thumb*, and demonstrated it to the builders of the Baltimore & Ohio Railroad at a time when they were purchasing only British locomotives.[174] Although he failed to convince the railroad owners to buy his steam engine, Cooper maintained his faith in the future of railroads and went on to build an iron foundry in Manhattan for the manufacture of iron rails and wire.[175]

By 1846, when Cooper was 55 years old, he estimated his wealth to be $385,500.[176] This amount distinguished him as an extremely rich man. He began to make plans to establish a great educational institution in the heart of Manhattan, which came to be known as Cooper Union. His generosity and knowledge of business and technology was fast becoming a legend throughout the young country.

Peter Cooper's politics were initially not much different from my own. He was a Jeffersonian Democrat but believed in "hard money." This view comported with those of the Northeastern industrialists, a class whose fortunes were rising at the time. It contrasted with the views of rural farmers who believed in "soft money." Soft money, unlike hard money, consisted of paper bills that were not convertible into specie. Soft money, according to the learned men of the science of economics at the time, was prey to inflationary pressure because only the steady backing of specie could counteract it.

Cooper's views on money would soon change, and eventually would markedly influence mine.

Chapter Fifteen – A Change of Viewpoint

———

A BOVE ALL ELSE, PETER COOPER HATED BANKS. Cooper agreed with Andrew Jackson on this subject and welcomed the latter's shutdown of the manipulative Bank of the United States. As a "hard money" man, he detested debt, high interest rates, and the "leveraging" of debt to expand one's capitalist holdings. Cooper endeavored in his business, in fact, to be wholly independent of banks. He preferred to be his own banker.[177]

During the 1830s and 1840s, Cooper did not maintain any bank account. Instead, he deposited all the cash from his businesses with Gideon Lee, an associate of his, every Saturday.

Lee was a merchant who later became Mayor of New York City and then a member of the U.S. House of Representatives from New York. Lee would keep Cooper's money each year until Cooper needed it. From that amount, Cooper would pay every bill by Christmas every year. Once he had paid his bills, he was satisfied to live on whatever he had left.

Cooper's personal life was not extravagant. He earned no interest on his deposits with Lee. When others were in financial crisis due to bank failures or credit crunches, Cooper remained a reliable source of cash for anyone who did business with him.[178]

While Cooper's financial methods managed to keep his head above water during the ruinous Panic of 1837, many other heads did not. Among those was another New York merchant named Edward Kellogg, a friend of Cooper's. Kellogg operated a dry goods store and owned real estate in Brooklyn. He was also an amateur economist. The Panic forced him to suspend his growing business. The experience induced him to think about the monetary system, particularly when interest rates reached usurious levels.[179]

Kellogg wrote a treatise and a book on economics that had a great influence on Cooper. The treatise, entitled *Currency, the Evil and the Remedy*, and the book, *Labor, and Other Capital*, advocated for "fiat money;" that is, paper money that is printed and controlled by government rather than by private banks.[180] These government notes, in Kellogg's view, would be backed by real estate rather than gold or silver, and would carry low interest. The notes could be exchanged for government bonds at the same low interest rate. Kellogg believed that this type of money would keep interest rates free from speculators and tie them to real economic growth.[181]

Kellogg's books greatly shaped Cooper's thinking about money. That, combined with his long experience in business, induced him to develop a theory of "managed currency." Rather than an easily-manipulated system wracked by inflation and deflation that was also aggravated by the enormity of America's debts to Europe, Cooper conceived of a purely domestic paper currency, controlled by the government alone and independent of convertibility into specie, that would adjust to the needs of the country and keep labor working.[182]

As the Civil War scaled ever upward in ferocity and cost, I was fortunate to make Peter Cooper's acquaintance while I was at Treasury and to hear his ideas.

PART FOUR
GREENBACK

Chapter Sixteen – The Rebel Encirclement

———

THROUGHOUT THE SPRING OF 1861, Washington City remained isolated and surrounded by hostile forces. The rail and telegraph lines to Baltimore had been cut; the Sixth Massachusetts Regiment that was making its way to defend the capital had been attacked by the Baltimore secessionist mob; and Washington was defended by only a small local militia and raw recruits from Pennsylvania.[183]

On April 18, before Virginia had even decided to secede, the federal armory at Harper's Ferry was overrun by the rebels. On April 21, the commander of the Norfolk Navy Yard ordered the facility burned before it fell to the Confederates. The federal troops and sailors there withdrew to Fort Monroe across the river at Hampton Roads, where they were surrounded by rebel forces. The Confederates invading the Navy Yard made off with tons of ordinance and ammunition.

I complained bitterly to President Lincoln about the disorganized situation on the battlefield under the command of General Scott and Secretary of War William Cameron. "All these failures," I wrote to him, "are for want of a strong young head.... General Scott gives an order. Mr. Cameron gives another. Half of both are executed, neutralizing each other!"[184]

Figure 27: The U.S. Capitol, May 1861 (New York Times)

At last, on April 25, the Seventh Massachusetts Regiment arrived in Washington and joined its companion, the Sixth, at an encampment on the unfinished construction site for the U.S. Capitol Dome. The next day, Union soldiers poured into the city, happily relieving us all from the danger of Southern invasion. Among them was the Rhode Island First Brigade, commanded by General Ambrose Burnside as well as the state's handsome young governor, William Sprague. He came from a family of wealthy industrialists in Rhode Island and would soon figure prominently in my own.

Chapter Seventeen – I Beg for Funds and Congress Delivers

———

C ONGRESS MET IN SPECIAL SESSION on July 4, 1861. The Republican Party, only seven years old at the time, held approximately eighty percent of the seats remaining occupied by Unionist Senators and Congressmen.[185] Lincoln's call to arms aroused the North, and sentiment for the Union was strong. The Northern banks rallied behind the U.S. Treasury and offered favorable terms for its bonds and stocks. The House and Senate passed, and the President signed, the most prodigious war budget in the country's history.[186]

Nonetheless, the financial health of the federal government at the outset of the war was precarious. As of March 7, 1861, when I took control of Treasury, the hapless Buchanan Administration had driven the government toward fiscal calamity. The public debt had grown from $64.8 million at the end of the previous fiscal year (July 1, 1860 to June 30, 1861) to $76.5 million. In the fiscal year of my appointment, which closed two months after that, it had grown by an additional $14.4 million. All told, the public debt had increased in the fiscal year before the war by more than 40 percent. By contrast, the balance of funds in the Treasury had dropped over that time by one-third, from $3.6 million at the beginning of the year to $2.4 million at the end.[187]

The government's budget that I faced for the coming fiscal year, from July 1, 1861 to June 30, 1862, was inundated by anticipated war costs. The total cost of the government in the last fiscal year of the Buchanan Administration was $84.6 million. But in the first year of the Lincoln Administration, it was expected to top out at *$318.5 million, an increase of 276.5 percent!*[188] War costs were expected to total $215.3 million, including $30.6 million for the Navy. These expected costs consumed 68 percent of the total budget.[189]

To cover this cost, I proposed to the July 4 special session of Congress to raise $80 million in taxes and $240 million in loans.[190] The taxes would guarantee the prompt payment of all ordinary demands of the government, including the payment of interest on loans and funding the gradual repayment of loan principal. But I knew full well that floating the enormous amount of debt that we had to undertake would depend on public's faith in the credit of the United States, which depended entirely on our Administration's prudent handling of public affairs, the punctual fulfillment of every public obligation, and the successful conduct of the war.

As for tax revenue, the federal government heretofore depended entirely on tariffs. It imposed neither direct taxes on the public nor excise taxes on goods.[191] But this approach would not do for what we faced now; the Treasury took in only $5.5 million in revenue for the last fiscal quarter before the special session of Congress.[192] We raised tariffs on all manner of previously-exempt and lightly-taxed goods, raising $27 million more than the $30 million that we had previously taken in.[193] Adding in $3 million in sales of public lands, we raised $60 million by the traditional indirect taxation method alone.[194]

I proposed to Congress $20 million in direct taxes and internal excises and duties for the rest of our tax package. We could raise between $20 million and $22 million by taxes on the value of real and personal property; or we could do the same by taxing stills, alcohol, tobacco, bank-notes, carriages, testamentary estates, silverware, and jewelry. I also suggested to Congress lowering the salaries of federal employees and confiscating rebel property that fell into our hands.[195]

Our biggest problem, however, was the enormous sum that we needed in the form of loans. I had only $21 million in borrowing authority left by the time that the special session of Congress convened. Much, much more authority was needed. I offered Congress two ideas. The first was implementation of a "National Loan," consisting of not less than $100 million. It would be issued in the form of short-term Treasury notes bearing interest at 7.3 percent per year, payable semi-annually and redeemable by the Treasury at its option after three years. Members of the public could subscribe to these notes at post-offices, banks, and through appointed Treasury agents in cities and towns throughout the country. The second was for a much longer term – the issuance to domestic and foreign lenders of $100 million in thirty-year bonds bearing 7 percent interest.[196]

On July 17, the joint session of Congress acted with dispatch on my recommendations. They authorized me to borrow $250 million, ten million dollars more than I had asked for. Only five House members voted against this authorization.[197] They authorized my "National Loan" plan in the form of bonds or Treasury notes of any denomination not less than $50, the bonds redeemable after 20 years and paying interest at no more than 7 percent; and the Treasury notes redeemable after three years and paying interest at 7.30 percent per year, which came to be known as "seven-thirty" notes. [198]Congress also authorized me to hire agents to sell the bonds. [199]

I was also authorized to issue non-interest-bearing Treasury notes of denominations less than $50 and as low as five dollars, payable on demand, which came to be known as "demand" notes. "Payable on demand" means that the person holding the note can ask for payment at any time, without being bound by a specific repayment schedule or timeline. I was also authorized to issue one-year Treasury notes paying 3.65 percent interest and exchangeable for seven-thirty notes.I was further allowed to negotiate $100 million in loans in Europe, and to issue $20 million in Treasury notes payable within 12 months and bearing six percent interest.[200]

Having thus authorized the necessary loans, Congress then appropriated $265 million for war and naval service as well as for civil and miscellaneous purposes.[201] This was more than enough to pay for my war budget, but federal civilian employees were considerably short-changed by having their salaries cut. Tariffs were also raised on a multitude of items – sugar, coffee, tea, molasses, brandy, wines, and silks.[202]

Each state, including the rebel states, was assessed a direct tax that would raise a total of $20 million, to be collected either by Federal revenue agents or by the states themselves as they saw fit.[203] Of course, the rebel states did not pay their shares. An individual income tax was also imposed for the collection of an additional $20 million.[204] This three-percent tax on annual incomes above $600, and five percent on incomes above $10,000, affected only the middle- and upper-classes.[205]

Everyone considered this gargantuan effort to be more than sufficient to crush the rebellion after the fall of Fort Sumter. But the people and the government were not mentally prepared for what was to come, and the effort so far proved to be far less than what would ultimately be required.

Chapter Eighteen – Reality Hits Hard

T HEN CAME BULL RUN.

Figure 28: Brig. Gen. Irvin McDowell, U.S. Army of Northeastern Virginia (PD)

For me, it was not only a setback for the Union – it was a personal embarrassment as well. I had personally advocated relieving General Scott from command and placing a fellow Ohioan, Brigadier General Irvin McDowell, in charge of the Union forces now in Washington. He ended up being trounced at Bull Run.[206]

On July 16, General McDowell crossed the Potomac with a Union Army of 36,000 men, the "Army of Northeastern Virginia." Both he and his troops were green, but President Lincoln assured him, "You are green, it is true, but they are green also; you are all green alike." [207] Thus "encouraged," McDowell and his troops entered Virginia.

A Southern spy network working in Washington, led by Rose O'Neal Greenhow, a prominent D.C. socialite, alerted Confederate General P.G.T. Beauregard of the movements and plans of McDowell's Army. Beauregard's "Confederate Army of the Potomac," 22,000 men encamped near Manassas Junction on the banks of the Bull Run River about 25 miles south of Washington, prepared a defense at a stone bridge over that river.[208]

Figure 29: Rose O-Neal Greenhow

Figure 30: General P.G.T. Beauregard, C.S. Army

Confidence in an impending victory for the Union Army was so high that many of Washington's elite social circles rode out to Manassas in buggies with their children to have picnics and watch the battle. Members of Congress tagged along with their families, toting baskets of food and wine.[209]

On July 21, approximately 18,000 men on each side clashed in and around the short stone bridge over Bull Run. The disorderly, incompetent battle turned by late afternoon into a Union rout. Almost 3,000 Union soldiers were killed, wounded, or declared missing. Some 2,000 Confederates were killed, wounded, or missing.

Union soldiers streamed in panic back to Washington, dropping their arms along the way. Frightened onlookers gathered their children and picnic baskets and hurried in their buggies along with the soldiers.[210]

Figure 31: Ruins of the Stone Bridge over Bull Run, circa 1865
(Photographed by George N. Barnard—PD)

The Confederates did not capitalize on their victory by moving forward to attack Washington. The North was shocked by the news. General McDowell was blamed for the loss and was dismissed from command, to be succeeded by Major General George B. McClellan. It began to dawn on everyone that this civil war would be a long, brutal, and costly affair.

- $ $ $ -

- $ -

A great weight now fell upon my shoulders to amass all of the Union's resources to prevail in this struggle. As General McClellan reorganized and augmented the armies and raised more troops, I began pouring out of the Treasury some $48 million a month to pay for the military's expenses.[211]

To meet these enormous payments, we hurriedly issued $14 million in two-year Treasury notes paying six percent annual interest. We issued $13 million more in sixty-day Treasury notes paying six percent. We also issued "demand notes," which we paid to our employees as salaries as well as to other Government creditors. Mr. Harrington and I agreed to accept them as payment for our own salaries, to encourage others to accept them also as their pay.[212]

At first, the demand notes were convertible into gold at the Treasury window after the three-year loan period had expired. But we suspended that privilege the following December. Merchants, bankers, and shopkeepers were reluctant to accept them at first. After a while, though, public sentiment turned and the notes proved to be acceptable forms of payment for all kinds of debts. By December 1861, there were $33 million worth of demand notes in circulation. [213]

One day in August, shortly after the disaster at Bull Run, I called Mr. Harrington into my office. "Mr. Harrington!" I said anxiously. "We are not selling bonds and notes fast enough! The demand notes will not cover our needs because of the resistance to accepting them in the marketplace!

"It is imperative that we shore up the Government's credit by insuring the reimbursement in specie of our notes and bonds. Our stocks of gold and silver are draining fast and we need to replenish them.

"The only way that I can see to accomplish this is to meet with all the Northern banks and get them to loan us money in specie. That will replenish our stocks of gold and shore up the Government's credit. How should we do this?"

Harrington, resourceful as always, had long before sensed what was now on my mind. "Mr. Secretary," he said, "we must hold conferences in all of the big banking cities with prominent financiers to raise the specie necessary for maintaining the Government's credit during the war effort, and to learn from them the best way to accomplish it."

"That would be New York, Boston, and Philadelphia," I said. "Would we meet with every banker in each city all at once?"

"I see no reason why not," Harrington replied. "They are fierce competitors of one another, of course. But when the chips are down for the nation as a whole, I think that they would rally to our aid out of absolute necessity."

"I think so too," I said. "See if the New York Subtreasury can help you arrange such a conference for the bankers there first. That will form an excellent model for Boston and Philadelphia afterwards. Perhaps in a couple of weeks?"

"I'll see what I can do, sir."

Harrington telegraphed the New York Subtreasury, and they in turn telegraphed all the major banks in the city. A conference was arranged for August 19, a remarkably fast turnaround.

There was a tremendous number of banks in New York at this time. Some 524 banks had formed there from 1790 to the beginning of the Civil War.[214] However, the New York banking establishment was not as large as this number might suggest. Eighty-six men served as an original director on more than one bank, 16 men were subscription commissioners on more than one bank, and one man had petitioned to open more than one bank.[215] It was imperative, therefore, for Harrington and me to meet with as many of these key gentlemen as possible.

Harrington and I traveled by train on the heavily-guarded railway through rebel-infested Maryland to the North. On Monday, August 19, 1861, we met with about fifty bankers at a long oaken table in a large conference room at the New York Custom House on Wall Street, which also served as headquarters for the U.S. Subtreasury.

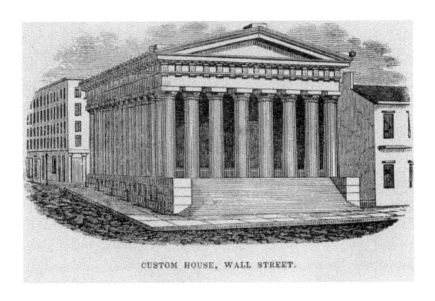

CUSTOM HOUSE, WALL STREET.

Figure 32: New York Custom House, circa 1861 (By Internet Archive Book Images[216])

After a few minutes of introductions and handshakes, the room became thick with cigar and pipe smoke. Tumblers of brandy, scotch and whiskey sat on coasters in front of every seat at the table.

Harrington and I didn't smoke or drink, and there was no way that we could encourage so many New York bankers to forego their essential pleasures for our sake.

"Welcome, gentlemen," I stood and greeted them. "I greatly appreciate the time you are taking from your busy schedules to hear me about the greatest exigency that this nation has faced since the Revolution. We are poised on the precipice of a dangerous and destructive civil war. I know that no one in this room wanted this war, nor did I most certainly, nor did President Lincoln.

"After Fort Sumter fell, everyone in the North certainly felt that the rebellion would be swiftly put down and that no other states would secede. Now, we have all come to realize that the country is so deeply split on the issue of slavery that we are willing to shed each other's blood over it.

"The sentiment in the North, however, is that states cannot secede from the Union. No matter what our social differences, we cannot and will not separate brother from brother in this artificial and unrealistic way. We will find a solution to slavery eventually, but it will be as a Union, not in pieces.

"This effort, however, will cost a lot of money. I have distributed to each of you a short financial statement of the Federal Government as of June 30, 1861, together with the revenues it has taken in and the expenses it has been incurring this year. It is a disturbing picture.

"To make a long story short, gentlemen, the Union needs a massive loan from you. We must raise an army of some 200,000 men to suppress the rebellion across thousands of miles of territory. We must build warships to blockade the entire Southern coastline of some 3,500 miles so as to stifle their foreign trade. We must field warships along the Mississippi, Ohio, and Missouri rivers in order to divide the South. As you are certainly aware, this will cost far, far more than a single foray of 20,000 men into Virginia, just to take a small stone bridge over an insignificant creek.

"For what we face now, we need a massive loan commitment from our nation's banks to see this crusade through to its conclusion."

"Mr. Secretary," spoke Benjamin F. Butler, a director on the boards of four New York banks, a Regent of the University of the State of New York, and a former law partner of ex-President Martin Van Buren. [217] "Please excuse the interruption, but I think this is a good time to express to you our collective take on this situation.

"All of us here are genuinely interested in seeing the government pull through this terrifying time," Butler said. "The Union is vital to our businesses. We cannot divide our assets and liabilities between two separate countries with two entirely different economic systems. We fully agree with President Lincoln when he said that 'a house divided against itself cannot stand.'

"We are, of course, ready to buy government bonds, but each of us can only take as much in bonds as our disposable capital will allow us to do. We are subject to stringent reserve requirements imposed by the State of New York. That limits our freedom to fund the Federal Government to the fullest extent of its needs. And we know that with every Union military defeat, especially one as disastrous as Bull Run, our ability to sell and distribute bonds to the public will slow to the point where they become almost worthless."

"I fully understand you, sir," I responded to Butler. "I am fully aware of what can happen if we have another disaster like Bull Run. But we have a new commanding general now, General McClellan, who I understand is a master at military organization and is just now engaged in organizing, with full Congressional support, the largest army that has ever been assembled on this continent. General Scott, before his retirement, proposed a grand plan to strangle the South like an anaconda by blockading its ports, and splitting the Confederacy right down the middle by seizing the Mississippi River. It will take time, gentlemen, but it will also take money! Lots of money!"

I was waving my arms in the air excitedly by this time in my speech. One of my hands almost hit Harrington, sitting next to me, in the head.

"Mr. Secretary?" John Dix raised a hand. He is a director of two New York banks, a former Secretary of State for New York, and an Adjutant General of the New York State Militia, which at this moment was serving duty in Washington.[218] "I feel that it is my obligation to inform you, sir, that several of us were very displeased with the way the Treasury Department handled its recent sales of bonds and notes. Although we were ready to purchase these bonds at their market values, you insisted on selling them for no less than six percent of par value. Their market value, however, was far less than that. There were other stringencies that you placed on the loan terms that did not sit well with us either. Is there some reassurance that we can have from you that you will work with us to ensure that the bonds you seek to sell are affordable and reasonably priced?"

"Mr. Dix," I responded, "I am certainly aware of your disappointment at the small discount on the bonds that you were allowed to take. But if high discounts were allowed as the banks were seeking, they would rapidly translate into high interest rates on loans that would weaken our borrowing power. High rates of interest during a period of national emergency are simply unacceptable. You cannot expect the government to pay inordinately high rates of interest or steep bond discounts when its back is to the wall. To me, that is simply immoral and unpatriotic. We are certainly willing to work with the banks to allocate risks between the people and the banks as equitably as possible, but the loans must be made on terms that we can accept."

Another hand shot up at the table. I must admit, I was starting to hyperventilate at the staccato barrage of questions being aimed at me by these august and implacable financial titans.

The hand belonged to William L. Marcy, a director of two banks and a former U.S. Senator. He was unimpressed. "Mr. Secretary, let me remind you that you are not in a position to dictate to us what the market commands us to bargain for. If you insist on terms and conditions and a rate of interest that we know the market cannot accept, we will simply issue you an ultimatum that you can take or leave."

This comment irked me. "No, Mr. Marcy. It is not the place of the Secretary of the Treasury to be handed an ultimatum, but to hand *you* one if it becomes necessary. It is our troops who are facing rebel bullets as we sit around this table arguing, not you and your clerks."

I realized that the point had come to get tough with these men. "If the banks will not accept terms that the Treasury deems to be reasonable," I warned, "then I will go back to Washington and issue paper notes for circulation that are not backed by gold. For it is certain that the war must go on until the rebellion is put down, if we must put out paper money until it takes a thousand dollars to buy a breakfast!"

The bankers eyed each other warily through the smoky haze of the room. I was threatening to inject inflation into the economy of such magnitude that whatever capital they held now would be worth next to nothing if they did not fund the war effort. *That* was something that they did *not* expect to hear from a usually-obsequious Washington politician!

"Mr. Secretary?" Mr. Butler spoke up again. "Would you be so kind as to excuse us to speak among ourselves before giving you an answer? I think that it will only take half an hour at most."

"Most certainly. Mr. Harrington and I will be in the office down the hall that is reserved for me."

"Thank you, sir. Much obliged," said Butler.

Harrington and I walked down the hallway to the office and sat in the chairs before the empty fireplace.

"Well, Harrington," I said, "what do you think?"

"I am sure that they know what a war will cost," Harrington replied. "They funded the Mexican War, and the War of 1812, and they provide funds to kings and princes for numerous European wars daily. They undoubtedly have a figure in mind that will match what you need. The only open question is what the terms are that they will extract from you."

"Well, they know damn well that they cannot fund the Confederates!" I spat out. "I doubt that they would get any better terms from the Confederates than they would get from us!"

"That, sir, depends on what the British are willing to do for the Confederates," Harrington said knowingly. "I can confidently tell you that that answer is 'nothing.' I have it on good authority that the British don't intend to throw good money after bad, either toward the Union *or* the Confederacy.

"Why, just last Sunday, the British agent in Washington for the London bankers called upon me after hearing about Bull Run about having his clients' 'little bill' attended to. He wanted me to give *security* for the payment of about $40,000 of the balance due! Well, I told him to come back on Monday, as the Federal Government probably would not collapse before the advent of business hours the next day!"[219]

We shared a good laugh on that one.

Just as we were chortling over the British gaffe, Mr. Butler stepped into the room. We stopped laughing and turned sternly to face him. "Gentlemen," Butler asked, "will you be so kind as to follow me down the hall to the conference room?"

We returned to the men sitting around the big table.

"Mr. Secretary," Mr. Butler said, "We bankers anticipated the demands of your visit today and we have spoken at length about what we expected you to say. We also realize that you plan to make the same pitch to our colleagues in Philadelphia and Boston and we've been in contact with them as well. All of us are willing to associate with one another to make you the following proposition.

"We will collectively loan the Federal Government $25 million, in the form of $5 million immediately, and the rest as you need it. What we ask of the Government in return is that the Treasury use its National Loan program to pay over the proceeds of its three-year notes bearing 7.3 percent interest to us in satisfaction of our advances, so far as those proceeds can go to pay off what Treasury owes us. As for any deficiency, we would agree to accept the same three-year notes at 7.3 percent interest to pay that off.

"Would you and Mr. Harrington like to ...."

"Raise the loan from $25 million to $50 million and you've got a deal," I said quickly. I knew that all I needed was a credit line that may or may not have to be called upon in the future.

Butler looked back at the conference table. Through the smoky haze, he could see that all the bankers were nodding their heads "yes."

"It ... looks like we have a deal, Mr. Secretary."

"Excellent!" I said. "And I take it that you speak for the bankers in Boston and Philadelphia as well, so that Mr. Harrington and I do not have to travel separately to those cities as well for the same $50 million?"

"That is correct, sir," Butler replied. "I speak for the banks of all three cities, and we are all associating for the purpose of making the Government this $50 million loan. Our lawyers will prepare the papers and send them to Washington within the week."

"Gentlemen," I said to all, "on behalf of the United States of America, I cannot thank you enough for this generous and patriotic offer. I believe that it will go a long way toward winning the war and saving our blessed Union!"

- $ $ $ -

- $ -

"I apologize, Mr. Harrington," I said to him as we rode the train back to Washington, "for not waiting to consult with you first before I accepted the banks' offer. Frankly, I would have taken anything that I could get my hands on from them and didn't want to seem small by haggling with them."

"Oh, you don't have to apologize to me, Mr. Secretary!" Harrington replied, smiling. "You just cut me off from shouting, 'My God, man, take it!'"

Chapter Nineteen – I Confer with Peter Cooper

———

ONCE BACK AT TREASURY, WE GOT right to work on the National Loan. Harrington and I hired 148 agents to distribute three-year notes in every city and town that remained loyal to the Union. They were paid a percentage of their collections. One agent in particular, Mr. Jay Cooke of Philadelphia, proved to be particularly adept at raising funds, selling fully one-fifth of the whole amount, for which he was handsomely compensated.[220]

Figure 33: Jay Cooke, circa 1892

The public was enthusiastic and snapped up the notes quickly. This energy was generated by patriotism, but not that alone. The public was *starving* for currency. Gold and silver had all but disappeared from circulation. Hoarding of gold and silver was rampant.

By mid-August of 1861, we had raised $45 million in coin from the sales.[221] We paid this amount over to the banks, along with five million dollars more in three-year notes at 7.30 percent to make up the deficiency.[222]

Figure 34: Brigadier General Benjamin F. Butler, circa 1862 (PD)

Ben Butler, who by now had convinced the governor of Massachusetts to activate the Militia and appoint him its head as a Brigadier General, marched on Baltimore and quelled the pro-secessionist riots there. He then had his men restore the railroad connection between Philadelphia and Washington via Annapolis, landing his troops at the Naval Academy and threatening pro-Southern shopkeepers who refused to sell provisions to his force. He warned them that armed men did not necessarily have to pay for their provisions and he would use all measures necessary to "ensure order."[223]

Butler and his fellow bankers were very pleased with our successful repayment of the $50 million loan on the agreed-upon terms, and consented that October to make a second $50 million loan available. [224]However, our second attempt at selling three-year notes did not prove to be as popular as the first. More Union Army defeats had followed, including Ball's Bluff, which greatly depressed Northern enthusiasm. We therefore ended the subscription campaign and delivered the notes directly to the bankers as compensation. Naturally, they were displeased.[225]

The banks were not forthcoming when I asked them for a third loan. In November, as military and naval expenses were piling up, I was compelled to issue six percent twenty-year bonds at a discount that enabled them to earn a return of seven percent. The banks took these bonds for $45.8 million in coin.[226]

Bank loans were paid to the Treasury in each bank's own notes, of course, unless they were paid in specie. The United States economy operated entirely on coin as well as the use of hundreds of different notes from its many banks, all of which were supported by the ability of the issuing bank to redeem their notes for coin. The banks were very eager to issue their own bank notes to the Treasury for use as payment for its expenses in lieu of its issuance of United States notes, including the "demand notes" that we were using to make direct payments of government debts. U.S. demand notes proved to be popular because they could be used to pay federal taxes, which tended to dampen demand for private banks' notes.

I particularly favored not relying on bank notes. I preferred to issue United States notes, relying on the credit of the people of the United

States rather than on the credit of individual banks. I did not want to give vendors the impression that the Federal Government favored any one bank over any other just because we used the former bank's notes. But the enormous expenditures of the Federal Government for the conduct of the war threatened to overwhelm the ability of banks to redeem their own notes with coin, because the government itself was absorbing all the available coin in the form of higher taxes and tariffs.

Eventually, it became clear to the banks that they could no longer redeem their own notes for what little coin they had, and they therefore universally and unilaterally suspended such redemptions as of December 30, 1861. They refused to redeem United States bonds and notes in coin as well. As a result of this action by the banks, the Treasury, too, had to do the same for its own notes in order to avoid a collapse in the value of banknotes.[227] This development threatened to disrupt the supply of provisions to our troops in the field.

By early 1862, it became clear to President Lincoln and Congress that the war would require the recruitment of *half a million men* into the Army and Navy. The war was forcing Congress to increase its yearly appropriations from $48 million in 1861 to *$214 million* for 1862, an increase of *346 percent*.[228]

I reported to Congress and the President on the need to adopt the most stringent measures necessary to reduce expenditures and raise more funds. I proposed the strict supervision of contracts; the abolition of government jobs; the reduction of government salaries; the seizure and forfeiture of rebel property; the increase of duties on all sorts of goods; and an increase in the direct tax being paid by the remaining states to the Union. I proposed to increase the income tax. All these measures required an enormous staff of revenue collectors, which of course we could not afford. Loans still seemed to be the only way, and banks were increasingly reluctant to grant them for fear of throwing "good money after bad."

- $ $ $ -

- $ -

One day in the winter of early 1862, as I sat in my office by the fireplace pouring morosely over revenue estimates for our depleting resources, Mr. Harrington entered.

"Mr. Secretary?" he said. "There is a gentleman here to see you. I'm sure that you know of him. He is Peter Cooper, of New York City."

Peter Cooper? The millionaire glue-manufacturer? What could this be about?

"Is there a federal glue contract that has gone astray, Harrington?" I asked.

Harrington smiled. "No, sir. He wishes to speak to you about something more important."

"Very well, show him in." I closed my books, dispensed with my piles of newspapers, and stood up from my easy-chair.

Harrington introduced us to one another and left the room. "Well, Mr. Cooper!" I said, extending my hand. "This is a surprise! What can I do for you, sir?"

Figure 35: Peter Cooper, Industrialist

"I am truly honored, Mr. Secretary, that you are taking my call," Cooper said modestly as we shook hands and sat in nearby chairs. "At the risk of sounding a bit presumptuous, sir, I have come to offer to you some suggestions for how to raise funds for the war effort."

What grace! I thought to myself. What a refreshing difference in character that this fantastically wealthy man shows compared to the Cuban-cigar-chomping, brandy-swilling, tough-talking Wall Street bankers I had to deal with only a few weeks ago!

"That is welcome news, coming from a businessman as distinguished as yourself, sir!" I replied. "Tell me. I always prefer informality in such meetings. May I call you Peter?"

"Why, of course! And may I speak to you on a first name basis as well?" Cooper asked. "May I call you ...er...Salmon?"

"I prefer 'Sam' myself," I prompted him. Peter appeared to be relieved.

"Thank you, Sam," Peter said. "I am here to speak to you about the possibility of establishing a national currency for the entire United States."

"A national currency?"

"Yes, a national *paper* currency."

"And what thing of value would we use to redeem this currency?"

"We would not redeem it with anything, sir. I believe that such a thing may prove very useful to paying the government's war expenditures."

I had heard some talk in Congressional circles about such a move, but as a "hard money" man I had always believed that currency was worthless to rational people unless it was backed by gold or silver.

"I wouldn't want to take up much of your valuable time, Peter," I replied, "if your idea is not predicated on an adequate means of converting such a currency into specie. Now that the banks and the Treasury have suspended the redemption of notes for coin, we are unable to fund the redemption of a new type of note."

"That is the beauty of my idea, Sam!" Peter interjected with sudden animation. "Redemption in coin for a national paper currency is unnecessary."

"If I were to pay my employees in a new form of currency, why would they accept it if they would not be able to go to the Treasury window and redeem it for gold or silver coin, which we know they trust?"

"The value would be established by government fiat, not by redemption in gold or silver," Peter replied. "Congress would simply pass a law. The law would establish the currency and its various denominations, and would declare that the currency is 'legal tender for all debts, public and private.' Therefore, people would accept it as payment for goods and services because they legally must. Otherwise, they are breaking the law!"

The United States used as currency only gold and silver coin up to that point, or notes issued by state-chartered banks that were redeemable "on demand" at that bank to the bearer in the form of gold or silver coin. The universal view is that notes used as currency must be redeemable in specie – either gold or silver coin – to have value as a unit of exchange. There would be no transfer of goods or services, I fundamentally believe, unless the object so exchanged for these things is itself a thing of value. Why would a merchant accept a mere piece of paper in payment for the sale of a genuinely valuable good or service that he has offered to the purchaser?

"Peter," I pointed out, "currency in this country is controlled by the states that charter banks. The Federal Government has nothing to do with that. As you well know, there was, at one time, a 'Bank of the United States' that was chartered federally, but President Jackson demolished it. So, our currency is a state-administered function, and our Constitution provides that the states may consider only gold and silver coin as currency. Thus, any notes issued by state-chartered banks must, by law, be redeemable in specie.[229]

"Even if the Federal Government were to issue currency as well," I continued, "it, too, would have to be in gold or silver coin. The Constitution empowers the Congress only 'to *coin* money.'[230] No one reads that power to mean 'to *print* money *on paper*.'

"Moreover," I added, "if we cannot convert our currency into gold or silver, then we cannot use it to pay our debts to creditors overseas."

"I know that, sir," Peter said, a tad testily. "We would not use such currency for overseas debts. We would continue to pay London bankers in specie, if they want it, or in pounds sterling, if they want that, or in drachmas, if they want that! Here at home, however, we would use the national paper currency solely among Americans, who, unlike Englishmen, must obey American law that treats such currency as legal tender."

I thought for a long moment. "Even if we could do this, Peter, wouldn't such a currency be susceptible to uncontrollable inflation? I'm fairly certain that experience has shown that too many bank-notes in circulation cause such calamities when there isn't enough specie to redeem them."

"But if I sell someone an apple, Sam, and he pays me with a bank-note, I do not have the time or inclination to run down to the bank and demand redemption of the note into gold coin. Instead, I turn around and purchase a banana with it. Redemption is then the problem of the banana-seller, not me. Chances are he won't redeem it either; he'll just use it to buy something else that *he* wants.

"Perhaps you have noticed, Sam, that even though the banks and the Treasury have suspended redemptions of their notes in specie as of December 30, commerce has not completely collapsed?"

"I suspect that merchants are just waiting out the banks and the Treasury to resume specie redemptions and will submit their stored-up notes later."

"Not at all!" Peter answered, with a big smile. "They are *spending* the notes on things that they need! The notes are circulating through the economy, even though they are irredeemable at that moment for anything other than the paper that they are printed on."

"I have always felt," I said to Peter, "that the exchange of currency is predicated upon things of value that merchants and customers are willing to accept in exchange for buying and selling goods. A merchant does not simply accept a piece of paper from a customer as payment when he has no idea whether he can enforce the payment in the form of a universally-valued commodity like gold. If the note is printed by a familiar bank, then he is assured that he can take the note to the bank and the bank will redeem it for gold or silver because the bank's reputation for having adequate stocks of such metals is well-established."

"A merchant accepts a bank note with the markings of a reputable bank stamped on it, Sam, but how is that different from a note printed by the U.S. Treasury stating that it is 'legal tender for all debts, public and private?' Bank notes have value because merchants know that they are redeemable in gold, but U.S. notes have value because the law that one must obey says that they do. One who accepts a U.S. note does not care about redeeming the note. He is only interested in using the note as a medium of exchange for goods and services that he wants, and *he knows that another merchant will accept it as payment too*, just as he has. He has no time to stand in line at the bank, during its limited hours of operation, for the sole purpose of exchanging all his daily earnings of bank-notes for bars of gold! He'll just give the notes to others as his payment to them for his debts to them."

"I see," I replied. I was beginning to realize that Peter Cooper had the gist of a laudable idea here. I had heard of this idea before, and had read a few scholarly articles about them, but until the present exigent circumstances, I had never possessed any reason to think seriously about them.

Peter was proving to be a hard man to shake out of his convictions. I tried one more approach to see if he had an answer to that as well. "But isn't it true, Peter," I asked him, "that we run a risk with unredeemable currency of having too many notes chasing too few goods, leading to inflated prices?"

"You do indeed, Sam," Peter readily admitted, with a slightly smaller smile than before. "But that is where the power of government comes in. If inflation starts to rise, all the government must do is to stop printing notes. Now I'm assuming here, of course, that the government will continue to accept the outstanding notes in payment of peoples' obligations to it, which means that payments in the form of taxes, tariffs, and other excises will eventually absorb a good deal of the excess paper money. The government would simply raise taxes and accept the paper money until the number of bills remaining in circulation are just enough to bring inflation down, without plunging the economy into *de*-flation.

"Now, the beauty of this, Sam," Peter continued, "is that the economy would no longer be imprisoned by the amount of gold or silver that it has on hand. We would not be held hostage to rich people who are hoarding gold to drive its price up. We would not have to worry that our economy will be jeopardized if gold flows out of the country to pay foreign debts, nor would we have to worry that countries with large gold stocks could starve us in the course of propping up their own empires.

"America is perfectly capable of feeding, clothing, and housing itself, and has all the natural resources that it needs right here to provide what our people need," Peter continued. "So, as long as we concentrate on our own needs and make all that our own people want, we can do so with a domestic paper money supply that we ourselves control."[231]

I was starting to become convinced by this profoundly erudite man. "Peter," I said, "you have quite a vision here. I am very impressed. But right now, I must fight a war. How does this ...vision ... help me?"

"You don't have to go to New York, Philadelphia, or Boston, hat in hand, to beg for money from banks, Sam," Peter replied. "*You just get Congress to pass a law making paper money legal tender for all debts, and then print as much paper money as you need.*"

This statement startled me. "How ..."

I never got the rest of my thought out of my mouth. Peter jumped right in. "Let's say you must build a warship. Congress appropriates $100,000 to build it. Rather than going to banks to plead for a loan that you would use to pay the shipyard in coin or bank-notes, you would skip that step and pay the shipyard directly with United States Treasury notes. The notes are, by law, 'legal tender for all debts, public and private.' They *must* accept them!

"Now, suppose they are reluctant to do so," Peter continued. "After all, they are hard-nosed businessmen who are familiar with banks, including dealing with the hard-nosed banks of London. Potentially, banks won't accept the notes themselves. Well, the only reason they would refuse to do so, Sam, is because they are *competing* with United States Treasury notes by the distribution of their own bank-notes.

"Well, Sam, if you face that type of lack of patriotism from bankers, you could make the United States notes redeemable for United States bonds, say bonds payable in twenty years at seven percent interest. By doing that, you are offering to make the paper money inflation-proof!"

Peter seemed to genuinely enjoy pummeling the banks in this way. "Businessmen always discount the value of money received over time by a certain rate of return. If you guarantee them recovery of that rate of return from the United States itself, then you are guaranteeing them that their money will never lose value because it is guaranteed by law. The banks can't do that; there is always a chance that they will go out of business."

"I see," I said. I was starting to wonder what the many hard-money men on my Treasury staff would think about this idea. Could I convince them that we might issue paper money without redemption in specie, contrary to our longstanding practice and worldwide custom, without making a mockery of myself in their eyes? Could I convince Congress? And the banks? And Lincoln?

Even more importantly, could I delay Peter from speaking to these people before I get to them? Where, after all, should the credit for shepherding American monetary policy lie, but here, at Treasury, with me?

"Peter, I am impressed with this idea. We are right now looking for ways to meet the enormous expenses of this war, not to mention saving lives. Let me discuss this matter with my colleagues in the Department. I will keep you apprised of what we decide to do."

"Excellent, Sam," Peter said, picking up his hat and coat to leave. "I will do my best to answer any questions that you or they may have. I bid you good day."

I called for Harrington to show the distinguished genius the way out.

Chapter Twenty – The U.S. Treasury Invents the "Greenback"

———

"**F**IAT MONEY?" HARRINGTON ASKED IMMEDIATELY upon stepping into my office once Cooper had departed. Harrington knew what the topic of our conversation was before I even told him.

"I take it that you are familiar with it?"

"It's been floating around here for quite some time. Mr. Cooper is a big fan of it."

"Are you a fan too?"

"Well, no," Harrington admitted, which I was relieved to hear. "I have a hard time getting my head around the idea that I could buy goods and services from someone and pay him with something that does not have any intrinsic value of its own. But I understand the idea behind this theory – he feels that the law provides the necessary "value" by obligating the parties to accept the paper as money.

"It is that a unit of exchange of any kind – bank-notes, gold, silver, wampum beads, anything that is a universally-recognized unit of exchange – does not need *intrinsic* value to be a recognized unit of exchange. It merely must be a thing that a buyer can give a seller in payment that the seller can then pass on to another in payment for something of equal value, and he to another, and so on.

"In a way," Harrington said to me, "it is not the value that the unit of exchange had *in the past* that makes it useful to the economy – it's its potential value *in the future* that makes it so."

This notion was still too radical for my mind to see as an answer to my problem of the moment – that I was fighting a brutal war and desperately needed recognizable money because my Treasury is empty!

"May I make a suggestion, Mr. Secretary?" Harrington asked. "As I'm sure you are aware, there is a great deal of resistance to this idea. We ourselves have a hard time accepting it. I'll also have you know that the banks are dead-set against it. But if there is one thing that I have learned in over twenty years working in the Washington bureaucracy, it's not the idea itself that wins adherents – it's the *organization which promotes the idea* that wins it.

"Now, at one time," Harrington continued, "the Federal Government came up with ways to unify monetary affairs nationwide. It formed the First and Second Banks of the United States. Congress simply chartered a national bank and authorized it to make loans and hold the Government's specie. But bankers of existing banks hated the Bank of the United States. That was because it was a *competitor* of theirs. And it was exclusively authorized to hold the Federal Government's assets, a privilege that they wanted for *themselves*. If *they* held the assets, they could make loans against it, and earn interest. So, they made friends with President Jackson, and he duly put the Bank of the United States to death. He then distributed all the Federal Government's specie to the individual banks.

"Now, it certainly wouldn't do to revive the Bank of the United States," Harrington said. "But what if the Treasury formed an *association* made up of itself and certain large banks that worked together to issue such currency? Treasury could be at the head of the association, but it would be administered by a 'board of directors' made up of officials from the largest banks. That way, Treasury could rely not only on its own resources and its power to tax, but also on the resources of the banks themselves."

"You mentioned '*largest* banks,' Harrington," I said. "Not *all* banks? If not, why not?"

"Oh, that's the beauty of it, Mr. Secretary!" Harrington replied eagerly. "Have the banks vie for membership in the association! Only the *largest* banks in the country would be allowed in! You could possibly regionalize it, so that the largest banks in every region could join, but the idea is to attach the Treasury to those with the most financial power as the way to accomplish the big things that we must accomplish right now."

"You know, Harrington," I said, "I have already gone on record with my last report to Congress against the "soft money," paper currency notion. But suggesting an *association* of the largest banks may be a way to get around the problems with paper money. The Government certainly hasn't enough credit with the people to create a national currency, but perhaps by allying ourselves with big banks, we could use *their* clout to do it.

"Can you have the Department put together a synopsis of this idea, and a suggestion for legislation?"

"Absolutely, Mr. Secretary," Harrington replied. "I should have it to you in a week."

- $ $ $ -

- $ -

Sure enough, one week later, I found when I entered my office that there was a 50-page printed report on my desk, replete with figures and tables. It was entitled:

UNITED STATES DEPARTMENT OF THE TREASURY

REPORT ON THE FORMATION OF

AN ASSOCIATION OF NATIONAL BANKS

"Well, Harrington!" I exclaimed to him that afternoon, when he entered my office after I had perused the report. "This is quite a piece of work in such a short time! Your department must have been working a good deal of overtime to produce this!"

"I have a staff of 50 clerks," Harrington replied. "It's amazing what these intelligent, well-educated young gentlemen can accomplish when one tells them what they must do to avoid conscription into the Army!"

- $ $ $ -

- $ -

The Report recommended the printing and circulation by the United States Government of uniform currency notes. It proposed the formation of a "national banking association" made up of nationally chartered banks that would be administered by the Treasury Department through an "Office of the Comptroller of the Currency." National banks would be subject to stricter regulations than existing state banks, such as imposing greater reserve limitations against lending too much. National banks would also help the war effort by acting as our agent to sell war bonds and other securities to the public.[232]

A "national bank" would be chartered as follows. It would deposit a capital reserve with the Treasury, whereupon it would receive a quantity of "United States Notes," printed by the Government itself, in proportion to the size of its deposited reserve relative to those of all national banks. To induce banks to issue United States Notes to the public instead of their own bank notes, Congress would enact a tax on notes issued by state and local banks. That usually tends to push non-federally-issued paper out of circulation.[233] National banks would be authorized to redeem United States Notes that they issued to the public, but only by means of United States stocks, bonds, and specie.[234]

Most importantly, the Report said, the United States Notes would be authorized by Federal law to be "legal tender for all debts, public and private."[235] They would be both retroactive and prospective in their operation, acting as payment for *past* debts as well as *future* debts.

After I finished the Report, I called Harrington into my office for a long talk.

"Mr. Harrington," I said somewhat warily, "I have always been a 'hard-money' man. I have gone on record several times with Congress and the people to that effect. Hard money, to me, has intrinsic value. It is gold, or silver, or notes backed by their redemption in gold or silver. Gold and silver coins weigh what they are worth. A gold dollar coin weighs the equivalent of one dollar's worth of gold by weight."

As always, dear Mr. Harrington excused my confusing circularity. "We are in complete agreement there, Mr. Secretary," Harrington replied, somewhat unctuously. He was happy to have a receptive audience, but I'm sure he was well-aware that it was a skeptical one.

"Now I understand this point, which Mr. Cooper also made to me, that declaring by *fiat* that a piece of paper is worth the same as a gold coin has the same effect on a merchant or a consumer as the weight of a gold coin itself. The law is the law, and one must follow the law. At the same time, gold and silver are inherently valuable, and no one doubts that they are worth their weight. Hence, both types of currencies can surely be used in any transaction to the same effect. If one refuses to accept a gold coin, he is inherently poorer for doing so. If one refuses to accept a 'United States Note' that is officially legal tender for all debts, public and private, he faces jail. The effects on the payee are effectively one and the same."

"Correct, Mr. Secretary!" Harrington remarked.

"But is it not true, Harrington," I continued, "that if one has gold in hand, he has *value* in hand; whereas if one has only *paper* in hand, he has only a threat of prosecution for not accepting it, which may or may not take place?"

"With all due respect, sir," Harrington replied. "that is actually a distinction without a difference. In both cases, that person has only one thing – *purchasing power* – in his hand. He will most certainly place the gold in a safe and remove it to buy something one day. As for the paper note, he will deposit it with a national bank, which will increase his account accordingly, and he will draw on it one day to buy something as well."

"I see," said I.

I pressed Harrington some more. "Well, this Report takes the concept one step farther, Harrington," I continued. "This idea seems to create a sort of shell game. We take 'real' value, in the form of reserves of specie, notes payable, or foreign currency, or whatnot, from certain very large banks, anoint those banks with the title of a 'national bank,' and thereby bestow upon them some form of *cachet* that is supposed to impress their customers with their power and soundness. They, and only they, can then issue 'U.S. Notes,' which have some magical power of being able to buy eggs and candles.

"Yet when someone goes to the 'national bank' to turn in that U.S. Note in return for 'real money,' all he gets are 'United States Bonds' entitling him to wait still longer for redemption, maybe with interest and maybe without.

"Aren't we just fooling the noteholder about the value of his money for a period, with nothing more than a promise to pay him back someday?"

"No, Mr. Secretary!" Harrington leaned forward in his chair toward me. "We are not fooling him. The first user of the U.S. Note uses it to buy eggs, say. The merchant who sold him the eggs turns around to buy nails that he can later sell in his general store, using the U.S. Note that the egg-buyer gave him, to pay for the nails. The U.S. Note discharges both debts instantly. So, when it comes to the marketplace, the U.S. Note serves the same purpose as a sack of gold dust.

"But as for the noteholder who saves the U.S. Note, the sack of gold dust that must be kept in a safe is simply replaced by an account entry at a national bank to the effect that he is richer by the face amount of that U.S. Note. Banks already do this accounting, only they must *also* store gold and silver in large, secure safes as well. These are eliminated by simple reliance on the accounting system alone."

Harrington emphasized his point. "It's *future purchasing power* that gold, silver, notes, bonds, and stocks represent, sir! It's not merely intrinsic value."

"Are we to assume, then, that bank panics will never happen again, Mr. Harrington?" I retorted. "What happens if we lose this war?"

Harrington thought for a long moment, then cleared his throat and spoke. "Of course, we may lose this war, and our U.S. Notes may then become worthless. The bank's accounts would also become worthless.

"But it is impossible to get along without this plan, sir. After all, let's be optimistic; we may *win* this war. We may neither win *nor* lose, but fight this war to a draw, and reach some understanding or treaty or truce with the Confederates. No one knows now what will happen when this war ends, Mr. Secretary.

"When the Revolutionary War ended," Harrington continued, "the states were bankrupt. They owed fortunes to the financiers who had bankrolled their war expenditures. How did the states repay the debt? Well, they formed a new government. They wrote a new Constitution and had the new government assume their debts. Did anyone at that time think that the new Federal Government would be able to pay those debts? Of course not! We could have broken up within months of signing the Constitution and everyone was well-aware of that! But people had faith, Mr. Secretary. There was nothing else to believe in.

"We must summon up that same faith now, Mr. Secretary!" Harrington said, gently pounding a fist on the arm of his chair. "It is the only thing that will sustain us every day that this war goes on."

Harrington was becoming a little strident in defending his report, but he was convincing. We all felt at that point that the world was toppling upon us, and we indeed had nothing to hang onto. The Treasury would be exhausted in less than 50 days.[236]

There was no solace from the battlefront or from abroad. We had just gone through an embarrassing incident with Great Britain that came to be known as the "Trent Affair." On November 8, 1861, our warship *San Jacinto* intercepted the British mail-steamer *Trent* near the Bahamas. The *Trent* was carrying as passengers two emissaries from the Confederate Government, James Mason and John Slidell, who were making their way to England. The crew of the *San Jacinto* seized Mason and Slidell and transported them to imprisonment in Fort Warren, located in Boston Harbor.[237]

The capture enraged the British. They nearly declared war on us. They sent a special messenger to Washington with instructions to seek not only the Americans' release of the prisoners, but to formally "apologize" to the British government, all within seven days. President Lincoln, anxious not to open a new front with the British, promptly rendered up Mason and Slidell within six days of the request.[238] It was an utter embarrassment for our country on the world stage.

We had little to show for our herculean efforts on the battlefield so far. Secretary of War Simon Cameron proved to be incompetent at his job and was dismissed. Edwin Stanton took his place. We then had some victories in the West: Fishing Creek, the captures of Forts Henry and Donelson, and Roanoke Island. But General McClellan and his vast Army of the Potomac remained immobile. The rebels held steadfast.

It was already apparent to me that we had to do *something* akin to creating wealth out of thin air!

Chapter Twenty-one – "When I Feel the Heat . . ."

HAVING WARNED CONGRESS ALREADY OF THIS FISCAL predicament, my opposition to the idea of paper money was not discouraging them from warming quickly to it. Representative Elbridge Gerry Spaulding, a Republican from Buffalo, New York, came to visit me during the late winter of 1862 to emphasize that view to me.

Figure 36: Representative Elbridge Gerry Spaulding of New York (PD)

"Why is it, Mr. Secretary, that you won't simply issue United States notes for exactly the amount that the Treasury needs without raising taxes?" the Congressman complained. "The notes should be interest-free and set by law to constitute legal tender for all debts both public and private, and should be deemed payable to the Government for any amount owed to it. That way, the economy can go on as before, perhaps with some inflation, but we can manage that by withdrawing notes from circulation.

"There is simply no need to burden the public with immediate and heavy taxation when paper money will do to run the war effort," he said. "We cannot run the risk of angering the people by imposing such burdens on them that will render them penniless."[239]

"We are indeed looking into the *fiat* money concept, Mr. Congressman," I replied, offering Spaulding some encouragement. "I realize that we would benefit from having a uniform currency throughout the United States and relieving ourselves of having to pay interest that way."

I hedged my encouragement, however, with some words of caution. "But the fluctuation in the value of paper money is a big problem for us. During a time of war, there is a great danger of financial panic that arises whenever there is a defeat on the battlefield, and overexuberance on every victory. Assuring that notes are convertible into gold and silver coin is essential to maintaining a constant value of such money. Our currency must continue to be redeemable for specie to keep the public's trust."

"But you have not even done that!" Spaulding retorted. "Neither Treasury nor any bank in the United States is redeeming notes for specie now! You have run up our national debt to the stars, and there isn't enough gold and silver in the entire United States to repay it. If we did *not* have to repay it, and merely relied on paper money that is exchangeable for goods and services by *fiat*, the Government would owe neither gold, nor silver, nor interest! I can tell you for a fact there is no political will in Congress to raise taxes as high as you have proposed, Mr. Secretary."

"As I said, Mr. Congressman," I replied, not wanting to tip my hand at what we are already looking into, "we are studying this issue and will soon release recommendations for a bill to ease the need for payments in specie throughout the economy. But bear in mind, sir, that the banks are not enthusiastic about giving up their tried-and-true ways of business in favor of a national paper currency, and we must come up with a way to induce them to go along with whatever we come up with."

"Well, then, get on with it, Mr. Secretary! Good-day!" Spaulding said as he plopped his stovepipe hat on his head, got up from his chair, and turned to go.

- $ $ $ -

- $ -

As the Congressman exited my office, I was reminded of an old saying here in the Nation's Capital: "When I feel the heat, I see the light."

In time, I came reluctantly to the conclusion that legal tender is a necessity, but I came to it decidedly and I supported it earnestly. [240] I authorized Harrington (now promoted to the position of my Assistant Secretary of the Treasury) to have a go at introducing a "Legal Tender Bill" in Congress.

House Bill No. 240, introduced on January 29, 1862, was entitled "An act to authorize the issue of United States notes, and for the redemption or funding thereof, and for funding the floating debt of the United States."[241] It was introduced in the House Committee of Ways and Means, in accordance with the Constitution's mandate that "All Bills for raising Revenue shall originate in the House of Representatives."[242] A speech in support of the bill was made on the floor of the House by Congressman Spaulding. Recognizing the fear many held that paper money would drive gold and silver out of circulation altogether, bringing our economic system to a halt, Spaulding offered this assurance:

> *It is a war measure; a measure of necessity and not of choice, presented by the Committee of Ways and Means to meet the most pressing demands upon the Treasury, to sustain the army and the navy until they can make a vigorous advance upon the traitors and crush out the rebellion. These are extraordinary times, and extraordinary measures must be resorted to in order to save our Government and preserve our nationality.*[243]

One month later, on February 25, 1862, Congress and the President acted and the bill became law. It came to be known as the "Legal Tender Act." It authorized the issue of $150 million in United States Notes. They bore no interest, and were issued by the Treasury in denominations of not less than five dollars each. Sixty million dollars' worth of "demand notes" that we had issued in July 1861 and February 1862 were retired from circulation as quickly as possible and replaced by an equal quantity of United States Notes. To assure the public that the U.S. Notes would be honored by the Federal Government when the present emergency had passed, they were made redeemable after five years for U.S. bonds having terms of 20 years and paying six percent interest. And as we still expected foreigners to pay our tariffs on their goods in gold or silver coin and not these notes, we likewise promised bankers that Federal loan interest would similarly be paid to them only in gold or silver coin.

The U.S. Notes appeared thus, and the green-colored design on the back quickly earned them the popular title of "Greenbacks:"

Figure 37: The $5 "Greenback" U.S. Note—Front and Back (PD)

The front of the note was adorned with the Statue of Freedom and a portrait of Alexander Hamilton, the first Secretary of the Treasury. As stated on the green back of the note, they were to be received in payment of all taxes, internal duties, excises, debts and demands of every kind due to the United States, except for duties on imports that had to be made in gold or silver coin; and were to be accepted as payment of all claims and demands against the United States of every kind whatsoever, except for interest upon the public debt, which was to be paid in gold and silver coin. The most important statement on the green back is what made the paper a currency: they were to be "lawful money and a legal tender in payment of all debts, public and private, within the United States," other than the payment of tariffs and interest on the public debt.[244]

These United States Notes turned out to be a huge success. They filled a yawning economic need for a cash unit of exchange on which commerce could rely in the face of the disappearance of gold and silver from the marketplace. No sooner had the Greenbacks hit the street than consumers and merchants started using them for the purchase of goods and services. They eagerly sought out the Greenbacks with which to pay their taxes and other excises. They were discounted somewhat next to specie, but the discount amounted to only three cents on the dollar.

The Greenbacks were so well-received by the public, in fact, that I asked the Congress on June 7, 1862 for authority to issue $150 million more U.S. Notes, this time in denominations of less than five dollars because of popular demand for notes in smaller denominations. This law came to be known as the "Second Legal Tender Act."

I came to realize that these U.S. Notes not only had monetary value for the public, but political *cachet* for me should I eventually decide to run for President again. The engravers encouraged me to add a portrait of myself to the bills, blandishing me with compliments of how good-looking I was.

So, I paid a visit to the studio of Henry Ulke, one of Washington's best-known photographers. He greeted me warmly and I explained what we sought to do.

"Most certainly, Mr. Secretary!" Ulke replied. Are you prepared to have the photograph taken now?"

I was dressed in my usual business attire and my usually messy hair was trimmed and well-combed. "Why, yes, I think I am ready now. Do you have any recommendations as to what I should do before you take the picture?"

"Nothing at all about your appearance, sir. You are a very distinguished-looking fellow, if I may say so myself."

Mr. Ulke led me to a room in the back of the studio. A ceiling window made the room very bright. His camera was set up at one end, and an elaborate chair on a dais faced it, with a small table supporting a book next to it. Behind were curtains and a false Doric column.

"Please have a seat, Mr. Secretary."

I sat, and Ulke experimented with different ways of facing me in profile, directly, or part-way in between. We settled on a slight smile on my face as the right pose, a one-third view, and crossed arms to suggest the strength of support that the Treasury was giving to its currency.

I was quite pleased with the result. I was handsomer than I even realized. Harrington had an engraving made to put the picture on the one-dollar bills, which appeared thus:[245]

Figure 38: The $1 "Greenback" U.S. Note—Front and Back (PD)

Chapter Twenty-two – Greenbacks "Win the War"

―――

I THINK IT IS SAFE TO SAY UNABASHEDLY THAT, in a way, Greenbacks "won the war." That is not meant to detract in any way from the bravery and sacrifice of our fighting men of the Union Armies and Navy. I say it only because Greenbacks provided the means to provision those men and thereby achieve their victories. The very different experience of the South during the war, which fielded equally brave soldiers on the battlefield, proves this to be true.

Our success with the Legal Tender Acts was followed in February 1863 with the enactment of the "National Banking Association" that Harrington's paper had recommended to me. It had not been passed with the First and Second Legal Tender Acts the year before because lobbyists for the state banks, fearing competition from the newly chartered National Banks, had it killed in the House Ways and Means Committee. By the following winter, Congress had begun to catch on to the idea.[246]

Entitled the "National Currency Act," the law enacted a single national currency for the entire United States, and taxed notes issued by state and local banks for the express purpose of pushing them out of circulation. The office of "Comptroller of the Currency" was established within the Treasury Department, with the express power of chartering "national banks" and regulating them. "National banks" were required to deposit a certain percentage of their capital with the Comptroller as reserves, and they were required to report their lending activities regularly to the Comptroller.

The national banks were empowered to issue demand-notes in proportion to each bank's level of reserves on deposit at the Treasury. They were also authorized to sell war bonds and securities in support of the war effort.[247] The demand-notes issued by the National Banks could be freely bought and sold on the open market. They were not, however, denoted to be "legal tender" that could be used as immediate payment for goods and services, as were the Federally-issued Greenbacks.[248]

By far, the most influential proponents of Greenback currency were our hundreds of thousands of Union soldiers and sailors in the field, who were paid their salaries in that currency. They used Greenbacks to provision themselves and they sent Greenbacks back to their families to use. Northern merchants readily accepted the notes from soldiers and their families to show support for our courageous boys in blue, fighting to save the Union. Southern merchants accepted them too in the areas occupied by Federal troops, where the Confederate dollar was worthless. Hoarding gold almost became a sin!

By March 1863, our currency circulation was buoyed by $450 million in Greenbacks, $400 million in three-year Treasury notes bearing interest at six percent (which were freely transferable to new owners), and $400 million in three-year Treasury notes bearing interest at seven and three-tenths percent (which were also freely transferable).[249]

I can best depict the expansion of our currency in the early parts of the war by the following chart, which shows the growth of legal-tender notes and the public debt as of June 30, 1862 and 1863:

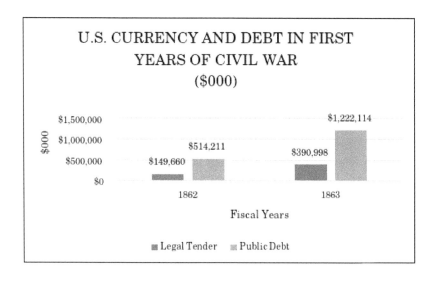

Figure 39: The Growth of the Greenback Currency and the Public Debt

Many have speculated about why the Greenbacks were so successful and widely-accepted by the economy, compared to "demand-notes." I believe that the latter were discounted by the public because they did not believe the "promise" made by the notes that they would be redeemable in gold or silver at some far-off later date. That would require the user to speculate as to the value of gold or silver at that later date – would it be greater or less than a demand-note was worth now? That, to each person, depended very much on his perception of the fortunes of the war.

With Greenbacks, there was no need to speculate. They were worth their face-value, *now* and *in the future.* They bought apples at today's price for the face-value amount of the Greenback, not by some discounted value of a demand-note. This fact greatly reduced fluctuation in the value of the currency.

The great concern about Greenbacks was their susceptibility to inflation. But that did not seem to worry the buying public.[250] Inflation worked too slowly to seriously affect creditors, who could readily adjust by altering interest rates. Wage-earners were scarcely affected at all, because the exigencies of war-time induced employers to raise wages by the rate of inflation each year to compensate their valuable workers for the loss. Pensioners and annuitants suffered the most because of the fixed nature of their incomes, but not too greatly. Nonetheless, the increase in business activity resulting from the expansion of the currency beyond what a gold or silver standard would have tolerated more than made up for these deficiencies.

As the Greenback was used domestically only, and not in foreign markets, its inflation was influenced more by factors of domestic supply and demand rather than foreign policy or the exigencies of war. Except for Maryland and part of Pennsylvania, the war was kept very far away from the urban North and did not disrupt markets there as devastatingly as it did in the South. The fortunes of war were reflected, instead, in the gold market itself, where prices would rise and fall in response to news from the front.

Gold coin is subject to "Gresham's Law," a long-standing theory that so-called "bad money" drives out so-called "good money." Bad money is a euphemism for paper money and "good money" is a euphemism for gold coin. When bad money circulates at the same time as good money, the good money fetches a premium over its face-value that induces its holders to melt it down and sell the gold at a profit. Good money is hoarded rather than circulated as a result, and therefore tends to disappear from the marketplace, leaving only "bad money" in circulation.

Union defeats and victories throughout the war tended to be reflected in rising and falling premiums of good money – that is, gold coin – as a percentage over their face-value, which was all that Greenbacks were worth. The course of this premium over time as can be seen from the following chart:

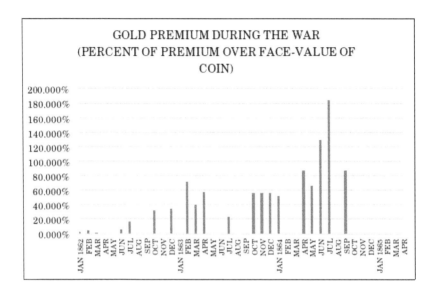

Figure 40: Gold Premium Over Face Value During War

The chart demonstrates that there were no great fluctuations in the gold premium throughout the early phase of the war, but it rose most steeply in 1864 because of the ferocity of the battles fought in that year as well as other factors, which I will get to presently.

The increase in the public debt was of much greater concern. But that was not caused by Greenbacks, which did not count as "public debt" *per se*. Being legal tender, any debt that was satisfied with Greenbacks was automatically discharged. "The buck stopped with the Greenback," so to speak. The public debt, by contrast, resulted from the enormous amount of long-term borrowing that the

Government had to incur to meet war expenditures. This debt could not be financed entirely by Greenbacks, for to do so would enormously expand inflation and depress the confidence of the banks in the Government's fiscal soundness. Bankers wanted to see that the Government was a responsible and steadfast borrower, which meant that it made its loan re-payments on time. Consequently, loans remained necessary to keep the banks content.

Figure 41: A Confederate Ten-Dollar Bill

The experience in the South was quite different. The Confederates, too, issued paper money, but they limited their issuances to demand-notes. They did not issue a *fiat* currency that was legal-tender for all debts, public and private. The Confederate paper dollar was accepted as a promise of that government to pay the face-value of the bill "six months after the ratification of a Treaty of Peace between the Confederate States and the United States."

This bill suffered from the same devaluation problem of our U.S. demand-notes, but with an extra wrinkle. Many people of the Confederacy were not in favor of creating a separate country that was independent from the United States. At least three-quarters to half of the populations of the Confederate states were "Unionists" who simply wanted to reconcile the slavery issue and keep the whole country together.[251]

Factions in the South broke away from the Confederacy and adhered to the Union, particularly in western Virginia, eastern Tennessee, and northern Missouri. The notion expressed on the currency itself of redeeming the notes after concluding a "Treaty of Peace" between the Union and the Confederacy did not resolve definitively whether the war would result in two countries instead of one. Rather, the Confederate government hedged on that issue, which undermined public faith in the currency. Hence, the Confederate dollar was very unsuccessful, experienced enormous inflation, and became worthless as the rebels' military disasters piled up.

Chapter Twenty-three – The Tide Turns

———

MY SUCCESSES ON THE FINANCIAL FRONT were impressive, if I say so myself. But the troubles of the Union Army and the squabbles of its egotistical generals caused me great stress. They led me into damaging conflicts with my colleagues, and eventually with the President himself.

My greatest source of aggravation was the incompetence of General George B. McClellan, Commanding General of the Union Armies, and head of the Army of the Potomac, serving in eastern Virginia. I shared this view of McClellan with General John Pope, who in midsummer of 1862 had been placed in command of the Union Armies in the Shenandoah Valley. He dined with me that July.

Pope railed to me about McClellan's incompetence and indisposition to active movements. McClellan was no match for Robert E. Lee, Pope said. In fact, Pope told me that "if, in my operations, McClellan should need assistance, he could not expect it from me."[252]

The new Secretary of War, Edwin Stanton, proved to be of great help to the Union effort, and to me as well. Both Seward and I had recommended him for the job to President Lincoln as a good lawyer and full of energy. Seward had also personally witnessed many of Stanton's administrative skills. Within only a few weeks of joining the War Department, Stanton had improved efficiency tremendously.[253]

Shortly thereafter, General McClellan began promoting a grand plan for a joint Army-Navy operation to capture the Confederate capital of Richmond by way of the peninsula between the York and James Rivers that emptied into the Chesapeake Bay. I opposed the plan, and so did Lincoln. The President thought that a direct overland assault on the Confederate army at Bull Run would be more effective. But, after hearing McClellan's grand and detailed strategy for the campaign, Lincoln reluctantly agreed to go ahead with it. [254]

Figure 42: General George B. McClellan, circa 1861, photographed by Mathew Brady (PD)

The implementation of McClellan's peninsula campaign was a ponderous and expensive affair. He took forever to move his enormous army into position. During that time, other generals were having great successes in the West – General Buell in Kentucky in January, followed three weeks later by General Grant's capture of

Forts Henry and Donelson on the Tennessee River, and shortly thereafter, General Burnside's capture of Roanoke Island.[255]

By June 1862, the peninsula campaign had used up our first $150 million issuance of Greenbacks that had been made the previous February, and the national debt began rising very quickly.[256] The General's constant demands for reinforcements and cash led Stanton and me to suggest to Lincoln that we should travel to the battlefield on the revenue cutter *U.S.S. Miami* to see for ourselves whether McClellan's demands were justified.[257]

While we were preparing for our journey, more important battles were fought while McClellan dithered. The Confederate ironclad *Merrimac* made its debut at Hampton Roads, destroying two wooden U.S. Navy warships. A month later, the Union's ironclad *Monitor* engaged the *Merrimac* in an inconclusive battle that drove the Confederate ironclad back up the James River. It was the first battle between two ironclads in naval history.[258]

Lincoln, Stanton, and I boarded the *Miami* at the Washington Navy Yard in early May 1862, bound for Fort Monroe, Virginia. The Chesapeake Bay was rough after a morning rainstorm, and Lincoln and Stanton took sick at the rolling breakfast table. I finished the hearty breakfast with no ill-effects.

We landed at Fort Monroe that evening. The President was anxious to visit the Hampton Roads Navy Yard, which was now in Union hands, and where the *U.S.S. Monitor* was now berthed. After that visit, we returned to the *Miami*. Lincoln was energized by the battle scene, and ordered the fleet to bombard the Confederate fortifications guarding Norfolk.

At that point, to our surprise, the *Merrimac* came into view. The *Monitor* sailed out to engage the *Merrimac* again. But to our great disappointment, the Confederate ironclad turned and steamed away, avoiding the battle.[259]

Now Stanton, Lincoln, and I were even more eager to see a real conflict. Lincoln and Stanton took off in a tugboat to see if they could find a suitable landing place for Union troops, leaving me on the *Miami*. However, when the troops landed there, they witnessed no action; the Confederate troops had retreated. Our troops then reached Norfolk, which had become an open city. There, the President met with a delegation of citizens carrying a white flag of surrender. They offered him a guided tour of the city.[260]

Having thus been thoroughly fired up by the "heat of battle," Lincoln, Stanton, and I returned on the *Miami* to Washington on May 12, 1862. I had now had an opportunity to observe Lincoln and Stanton at close range. My impression of Lincoln's military prowess improved somewhat. We returned to the Cabinet table in Washington, where future disagreements on the course of the war would continue to rage among us.

Figure 43: General Henry Halleck

Eventually, General McClellan was relieved as Commanding General of all the Union Armies and replaced by General Henry Halleck. Halleck was more knowledgeable about military affairs as well as more parsimonious than the extravagant McClellan; therefore, more to my liking. Also to my liking, he spoke fluent French, as I do.[261] But Lincoln still left McClellan in charge of the Army of Northern Virginia (as the Army of the Potomac was now called), a conciliatory recommendation of Halleck's to the President that displeased me greatly.

- $ $ $ -

- $ -

In time, the issue of slavery demanded more and more of the Cabinet's time. I had strongly urged the use of free blacks in the conquered part of Louisiana to take on a military role there. Halleck downplayed my idea, confessing to the President that "I do not think much of the negro."[262] Lincoln let the matter drop for the time being.

I was beginning to feel as if what I thought ought to be done was generally being left undone, and what I thought ought not to be done was being done. I started to doubt the value of my views on any subject in these Cabinet meetings.[263]

In late August, we received horrific news – General Pope's army was soundly defeated by Generals Lee and "Stonewall" Jackson in the Second Battle of Bull Run. Stanton and I, meeting in Stanton's office at the War Department after the telegram of the defeat was received, were devastated that our champion against McClellan was brought so low. Ironically, we were both convinced that McClellan's force could have rescued Pope from humiliation.[264]

"This is outrageous!" Stanton yelled, stomping around his office in a fit of apoplexy as I watched him. "McClellan is never where he should be when he should be! His army is marching around Northern Virginia like a bunch of martinets while John Pope gets massacred only a few miles away!"

Figure 44: Secretary of War Edwin M. Stanton (PD)

"McClellan is a menace," I said ruefully. "We have put this egotistical bastard up against men like Lee and Jackson, who run rings around his ponderous movements.

"We must get rid of him," I said. "What if we were to approach the entire Cabinet and form a united front to convince Lincoln to sack him?"

"The problem there is Halleck. He supports keeping McClellan because the troops love him. But I don't trust him. I do not think McClellan has his heart in fighting the South. I also think that he's scheming to run against Lincoln in the next Presidential election."

"Look, Ed," I said, "let us write a memorandum to the President that sets out McClellan's defects and recommends his immediate dismissal. You and I can sign it now, and I will take it to the other Cabinet members for their signatures. Then I will present it to the President."[265]

"All right, then," Stanton sat down at his desk, grabbed a sheet of paper and a pen, and started writing.

It took us all of an hour and a half to compose the draft and sign it. I left with the draft immediately to show it to Gideon Welles at the Navy Department.

Figure 45: Secretary of the Navy Gideon Welles

I caught Welles at his office door just as he was leaving to go home for the day.

"Gideon, I've just come from Edwin's office. We've drafted and signed a memorandum to the President. Please read this." I handed him the draft.

Sighing heavily as one would naturally do when being delayed from having a good dinner, Welles took the draft back to his desk, put on his reading glasses, and started to peruse the document.

Presently, he looked up at me with a frown and said, "I will not sign this. I would rather have the President ask me for my opinion and I would then give it. If he did, I would tell him that he should remove McClellan. But giving him this memorandum, signed by all the Cabinet Secretaries, would be highly presumptuous of us. It's the President's decision, not ours, to make."

"I cannot agree, Gideon," I replied. "The Cabinet must act with energy and promptitude, for either the government or McClellan must go down!"

"Have you shown this to Bates, or Blair?" Welles asked me, referring to the Attorney General and Postmaster General, respectively.

"Not yet," I replied. "Their turn has not yet come."

Welles did not ask me about Secretary of State Seward, whom we both knew was out of town at that moment.

"Well, at least go see Bates first," he said, "of any of us, he should be the one writing it." He grabbed his hat and headed out, leaving me behind.

The next morning, I went to see Attorney General Edward Bates. We were only now learning of the truly disastrous impact of General

Pope's defeat at Bull Run. Bates, like Welles and Stanton, was in full agreement with me that McClellan had to go. After reading the draft, he offered to compose a different one and signed it. I took it to Stanton and Secretary of the Interior Caleb Smith, both of whom signed along with me. I took this signed draft back to Welles.

"It's an improvement and less exceptionable," Welles said to me this time. "But it's disrespectful to the President to present him with this. I will not sign it. You cannot control him like this, when he is most vulnerable to attack."

"That is not my purpose!" I protested. "Look, Gideon, I agree with many of the things you've said about these drafts. But conversations amount to little with the President on subjects of this importance. Argument is useless. It is like throwing water on a duck's back. A more decisive expression must be made, and in writing!"

"I'm sorry that you feel that way about the President, Sam. I cannot sign it. I wouldn't want this draft to be floating around and getting discovered by the press, either," he warned.

- $ $ $ -

- $ -

The next day, at our regular Cabinet meeting, the confrontation came to a head.

I had the memorandum in my vest pocket, signed by myself, Stanton, Bates, and Smith. There were spaces for Welles and Blair but they were devoid of signatures. Seward was not listed.

It was the President who detonated the bomb. "Gentlemen," he said in his characteristic midwestern twang, "I've had a talk with General Halleck about General Pope's defeat at Bull Run. He and I have agreed that the remainder of Pope's army should be placed under the command of General McClellan.

"McClellan knows this ground well," Lincoln continued. "His specialty is to defend, and he is a good engineer, we all admit. There is no better organizer; he can be trusted to act on the defensive, but I readily admit to all of you that he is troubled with the slows."[266]

We all knew of McClellan's immense popularity with the rank and file of the army. None of us, especially Lincoln, was anxious to challenge him.

Blair spoke next. "I have known General Pope intimately for years," he said. "His defeat comes as no surprise to me. He was always a braggart and a liar, with some courage perhaps, but not much capacity."[267]

Figure 46: Postmaster-General Montgomery Blair (PD)

"Mr. President, I agree with Montgomery about General Pope," I said, "but as bad as he has turned out to be in leading his army against Lee and Jackson, you cannot ignore the fact that it was McClellan who ignored his plight and failed to move his enormous army into position to help him when he needed it.

"I am very wary of placing McClellan in charge of Pope's remnants," I warned. "I fear that it will be a national calamity."

"I understand how you feel about McClellan, Sam," Lincoln said, "but I need to make some serious changes in the command structure now that we see how extensive this conflict is turning out to be. McClellan handles the army far better than McDowell did."

That comment stung me, as I was the one who recommended McDowell for command of the army in the first place, only to see him replaced by McClellan after the first disastrous Battle of Bull Run.

I kept the memorandum in my vest pocket and never pulled it out for the remainder of the Cabinet meeting. Nobody else brought it up either.

- $ $ $ -

- $ -

Lincoln's next surprise came a few weeks later, at another Cabinet meeting.

There had been several developments in the middle of 1862 on the issue of emancipating the slaves. It had arisen early in the war, when General Butler, in command of Fort Monroe on the Virginia peninsula, allowed a group of fugitive slaves to seek shelter in the Fort and turned away a group of Southern bounty hunters looking for them. Butler deemed them to be "contraband of war," treated them as "seized property," and put them to work for the army while they lived in the Fort.

This act emboldened other Union generals to do the same. General David Hunter, who controlled the coastal areas of South Carolina, Georgia, and Florida, issued a proclamation freeing slaves in the area under his command. Lincoln, who considered emancipation to be a matter for the states and not the federal government, revoked the proclamation.[268]

Up to this point in the war, Lincoln had been in favor of awaiting state actions on emancipating slaves. He favored compensation for slave-owners who freed their slaves, and favored colonizing freed slaves outside of the country.[269] However, in late July, the President called an unscheduled meeting of the Cabinet, a day in advance of the regular one. He had prepared several draft executive orders for our consideration, one of which surprised all of us.

Figure 47: "First Reading of the Emancipation Proclamation by President Lincoln," painting by Francis B. Carpenter, 1864 (PD). Tellingly, Chase and Stanton are to Lincoln's left and the rest of the Cabinet (Welles, Smith, Seward, Blair, Bates) are to his right.

I started off the meeting by pleading General Hunter's case for enlisting, training, and arming liberated slaves. The General had written to Lincoln making this request because General McClellan had stripped him of his troops and he was put in a perilous position unless he could employ black manpower. I pushed the President for arming blacks as a military necessity.[270]

Lincoln listened patiently to me, and then quickly rejected my argument. He then started reading his executive orders to us, one of which called for the insurrectionary states to return to the Union "within sixty days" of its effective date. He offered compensation to slave-owners for emancipated slaves, as we expected, but then proclaimed the emancipation of "all slaves within states remaining in insurrection on the first of January 1863."[271]

I could not believe my ears! I could not believe that Lincoln, who like me had considered emancipation to be a matter within state control, would exercise his powers as Commander in Chief of the Armed Forces to free all slaves throughout the remainder of the Confederacy on a date certain! It was a brilliant military maneuver, of course – the slave states that had remained loyal to the Union were left to free their slaves on their own in due course, but the Union Armies would now be in the business of establishing freedom wherever they took control, and enlisting them in the Union Army!

I caught my breath, then smiled and said, "Mr. President, I second your proclamation most heartily!"

Stanton said, "I urge you to promulgate all of your orders immediately, Mr. President."

Bates, the most conservative member of the Cabinet, said, to my surprise, "I agree with Mr. Stanton."

It was Seward who then talked everyone down. "Mr. President," he said, "I strongly urge you not to issue that proclamation. As your Secretary of State, I must caution you that foreign nations would take it to mean that you intend to abolish slavery throughout the

United States and they will try to stop you. They want America to produce cotton for their mills. We are the largest producers of cotton in the world.

"If we emancipate the slaves of the Confederacy, we will shut down the cotton industry for good," he said. "India will take it over. England and France will recognize the Confederacy for the sake of preserving their cotton trade and will support our defeat.

"No one, North or South, wants this to happen," Seward continued. "Wait for our troops to finish the job of putting down the insurrection and leave it to our generals in the field and our state governments to end slavery."

I thought that I may have supported Lincoln's idea too soon. This was indeed a more rapid emancipation than any gradual plan that I or any of my co-abolitionists had contemplated. Surely, it was also a step that a federal government of limited powers might not have the Constitutional power to take. Still, the awesome power of the Commander in Chief of the Army and Navy encompassed many possible measures under the guise of "military necessity" that might not be attempted in normal times.

"I do not fear the hypocritical wrath of foreign powers who have already freed their own slaves," Lincoln responded to Seward.

Following some more conversations later in the evening, and after the Cabinet meeting had concluded, Lincoln let it be known that he would shelve his proclamation for a while. It would be better, he said, to wait for a Union victory somewhere before announcing it, so as not to make it seem like we were acting out of weakness and desperation, especially to foreign nations.

That September, the necessary victory finally came. General McClellan met General Lee at Antietam, Maryland and defeated him, albeit at an unimaginably heavy cost to both sides. Sadly, McClellan did not pursue Lee and his wounded army back into Virginia for the final blow.

Lincoln convened a special Cabinet meeting shortly thereafter. The Emancipation Proclamation was announced the next day, September 22, 1862:

> *That on the first day of January, in the year of our Lord, one thousand eight hundred and sixty-three, all persons held as slaves within any State or designated part of a State, the people whereof shall then be in rebellion against the United States, shall be then, thenceforward, and forever free.* [272]

THE PAST AND THE FUTURE.

Figure 48: The Past and the Future, by Thomas Nast, 1863 (PD)

Chapter Twenty-four – My Ascending Star Flames Out

———

T HE CABINET, AFTER ISSUANCE of the Emancipation Proclamation in September 1862, started coming apart at the seams. The unique personalities of the eight men in it started to grind on one another beneath the impossible pressure of this inordinately long, bloody, and disheartening war. Some jockeying in anticipation of the 1864 Presidential election also became evident.

After the costly victory at Antietam and the Proclamation's issuance, I fomented serious discussions in Cabinet meetings and among friends in the Radical Republican caucus about cashiering McClellan. His immobility and failure to pursue Lee into Virginia after the battle was viewed as snatching defeat from the jaws of victory. He was vilified in the Northern press for it. I was quite tired of McClellan's endless demands on the Treasury. I searched around for candidates among our now-experienced military establishment for an appropriate replacement.

There was Joseph Hooker, a brave general who had distinguished himself for dynamic action during the Peninsula Campaign, Bull Run, and Antietam. I visited him with my daughter Kate and Colonel James A. Garfield, now a congressman-elect, while Hooker convalesced at a Washington hospital from a wound he received at Antietam.[273]

My daughter Kate, ever charming toward men she admired, brought "Fighting Joe" (as he was now called) a basket of fruit, pastries, and similar fare. We were eager to hear what he might have to say about McClellan as his commander.

Figure 49: General Joseph Hooker

"How do you find General McClellan?" I asked Hooker as he munched on a sticky-bun.

"He's a fine commander," Hooker answered without looking at me directly.

"The President thinks that he seems to be rather afflicted with 'the slows,' as he puts it."

Hooker lowered the sticky-bun on his napkin and looked at me directly this time. "Well, Mr. Secretary, General McClellan is a very meticulous, deliberate soldier. He's an engineer, you know, and he insists on organization and defense in depth. I must agree with the President that McClellan has missed a great many opportunities to crush Lee and his army."

"You mean at Bull Run?"

"There, and even at Antietam. Lee and Jackson crushed Pope's force at Bull Run, but McClellan's huge army could have easily reached the scene and pursued them. At Antietam, it was the same thing – McClellan didn't go after them after the battle. Of course, we had taken such a beating there that we were probably too exhausted to prevail over them if we did."

In the carriage on the way home, I said to Kate and Garfield, "I like Hooker! I can see why his men call him 'Fighting Joe.' He's quick-witted, direct, and honest. He would make a fine substitute for McClellan!"

"Father, I would be very careful about that if I were you," Kate cautioned. "There are rumors spreading around Washington of a rift in Lincoln's cabinet, and you may be on the wrong side of it."

"Oh, really?" I replied. "I know that Stanton and I think alike. We cannot stand McClellan. Of course, we are the ones who have the most direct contact with him. The other Cabinet members do not, and they are by no means a cohesive body of thinkers on him."

"There are those who are calling you quite argumentative with Lincoln," Kate replied. "He is known for his patience, but I have heard that he can snap sometimes."

Figure 50: Kate Chase

It would have been wise of me to take my daughter's sage advice. It was not long before I found out exactly what Abraham Lincoln thought of me.

- $ $ $ -

- $ -

McClellan's army was motionless after Antietam. Republicans in Congress and Northern newspapers were clamoring for action now, to defeat the Confederacy while we had the upper hand. Stanton and I were among the members of that chorus, but Seward was not. The rest of the Cabinet was non-committal.

Figure 51: General Ambrose Burnside (PD)

In November 1862, I found out that Lincoln had removed McClellan from command and had replaced him with General Ambrose Burnside. I was disappointed in the choice, having preferred "Fighting Joe" Hooker over the less distinguished Burnside. But Lincoln did not consult either Stanton or me before making his decision.[274]

The divisive egos of our Cabinet members, and Lincoln's tendency to consult generals but not the Cabinet before making battlefield decisions, were driving us apart. I found myself frequently allied with Stanton against Seward for Lincoln's attention while the other members were more passive.

I found Seward to be rather gruff and arrogant. I preferred more ingratiating personalities. Lincoln, a known story-teller and jokester, felt comfortable with Seward, an old New York politician with an easy manner and many anecdotes of his own to amuse Abe with. I have always been a more reserved man.

In early December 1862, certain Radical Republican senators who were personal friends of mine, and to whom I had complained often about White House conflicts, caucused to create a committee to induce Lincoln to partially re-form the Cabinet. The nine-member committee, headed by Senator Jacob Collamer, approached the President for a meeting with the committee.[275] Abe scheduled it for the evening of December 19.

The senators spent three hours with Lincoln that night, complaining about the conduct of the war and primarily about Secretary Seward. They presented a series of resolutions that they had prepared to re-organize the Cabinet more to their liking. Lincoln did not react much to what the senators had told him, and instead called a special Cabinet meeting for the next morning.[276]

We all attended the meeting except Seward. He had heard about the caucus meeting with Lincoln and sent a messenger to him, declining to attend and presenting him with his resignation.

Figure 52: Secretary of State William H. Seward

The President informed us of what had transpired the previous night. He was uncharacteristically quite serious and appeared to be deeply troubled by this development. "This is very dangerous," he told us. "The senators are quite steamed about the progress of the war and the conduct of the commanding generals. They also are very critical of Seward, whom they consider too conservative.

"Bill heard about the committee and asked me to excuse him from this meeting, also sending me his resignation," the President told us, pulling an envelope out of his coat pocket. "I am very worried that this signals a lack of confidence in my leadership and could lead to a collapse of the government.

We here cannot let that happen," Lincoln continued. "However, I do not want anyone in here to take it upon themselves to resist the senators, whatever might be the termination of this affair. I would like all of you to meet with me again this evening to sort this out."

Unbeknownst to us, and unbeknownst to the senators of the committee, Lincoln had arranged for both the Cabinet and the senators to join him at the same meeting. He deliberately convened a confrontation between Cabinet members and the senators to express their differences and probe each other for solutions. Again, Seward was not in attendance.

When I arrived at the White House and entered the conference room where the meeting was convening, I discovered who was in attendance and felt instantly ill at ease. When the meeting began, Lincoln turned to me first.

"Secretary Chase, let me start by asking you whether, in your view, the Cabinet is divided on policy, as this committee charges?"

My mouth was dry. "Mr. President, gentlemen, if I had known that I would be arraigned before this committee this evening, I would not have attended this meeting. But since I am here, I must admit that there has been no want of unity in the cabinet, only a general acquiescence on public measures.

"I can only point out," I continued, anxious to downplay the conflicts while in Lincoln's presence, "that consultations with the Cabinet as a whole are infrequent."[277]

The senators, all of whom I had complained to personally and often about the Cabinet's woes, looked at me skeptically. "Is that all that you have to say, Mr. Secretary?" Senator Collamer asked.

"Y-yes, Senator," I stammered.

The other Cabinet members were similarly grilled, and all expressed the same sentiment that I did. The only difference was that the sentiment that I now expressed did not match the sentiment that I had expressed to them on other occasions when out of the President's earshot.

The next day, Stanton and I were summoned to the White House. As we stood in the President's office waiting for Lincoln to arrive, Gideon Welles walked in.

Welles seemed a bit surprised to see us. "What brings you gentlemen here?" He asked us.

Before we could answer, Lincoln walked in.

"Gideon!" the President said. "Have you seen the man?"

"Yes, Mr. President," Welles replied. "He has assented to my views."

"Good!" said Lincoln. He turned to Stanton and me. "That man is Seward," he told us. "I asked Gideon to go speak to him for me and see if he would retract his resignation. He has.

"Sam," Lincoln said to me angrily, "I sent for you, for this matter is giving me great trouble. Apparently, these senators have been hearing from you that there are rifts in my Cabinet that I cannot resolve. Last night, you told them the opposite and so did all the other Cabinet officers except Seward, of course. And apparently, they were even led to believe that Seward was the cause of this supposed rift, and when Seward heard of it, he was so distraught that he offered me his resignation! Fortunately for me, he has now rescinded it."

I was sorely shaken by the President's tone toward me. "Mr. President," I stammered, "I – I was painfully affected by the meeting last evening, which was a total surprise to me. I am prepared to offer you *my* resignation. I - I have it right here in my pocket."

"Let me have it!" Lincoln barked. I held out the envelope and he snatched it from my hand, ripped it open and read it.

He laughed and turned to Welles. "This cuts the Gordian knot, Gideon! I can dispose of this matter now without any difficulty! The trouble is ended!"

Stanton, seeing what was taking place to me and sensing his own vulnerability by association with me, said seriously, "Mr. President, I, too, will offer you my resignation. I have agreed with Sam's sentiments on McClellan and Seward for quite some time."

"I don't want yours!" Lincoln turned on him. "Good day, gentlemen." Lincoln left the room. After he had gone, the rest of us left as well, without so much as even saying "goodbye" to one another.[278]

I returned to my office quickly, in a total panic. I was completely embarrassed in front of Senators who were my friends and had let down the President with my unintentionally seditious behavior. As

I entered my office, I found John Nickolay, the President's secretary, waiting there for me.

"Mr. Secretary?" He said, "I have a note for you from the President."

Apprehensively, I opened it. It was addressed to Seward and myself. It requested us to take back our resignations and "resume the duties of your Departments respectively." It was signed, "A. Lincoln."

I heaved a sigh of relief. Evidently, my services to the country were more important to Lincoln than his personal feelings, which encouraged me. When I later received a note from Seward that he had rescinded his resignation as Welles had reported, I replied to Lincoln's note somewhat smugly that I would "sleep on it." Over the weekend, I wrote a long letter to the President rescinding my resignation, but reiterating my now-outed feelings about his conduct of the Cabinet.

Despite my personal relief, I now stood as a man under suspicion in the Cabinet and disgraced in front of my friends in the Senate. My mind wandered back to my decision to put my portrait on the one-dollar Greenback. "How stupid of me!" I muttered to myself. Lincoln probably felt upstaged by my self-centered move to place my face on it instead of his own. After all, he was the President, not me! That thoughtlessness on my part undoubtedly had more to do with his anger at me than the senators' complaints about Seward.

Chapter Twenty-five – My Time at Treasury Comes to a Close

———

A LTHOUGH MY STAR WAS FALLING in the eyes of the President, it was rising in many other political corners, beckoning me toward a run of my own for the Presidency in 1864.

I engaged in an extensive round of speechmaking through Ohio and Indiana in advance of the off-year elections of 1863. Greenbacks were rescuing the economy of the country. Congress saw fit in 1863 to pass yet a third Legal Tender Act, extending the circulation of Greenbacks by an additional $150 million.[279] My national banking system was being well-received by the financial world. We also received from Congress additional borrowing authority and increased excise taxes and tariff duties, all of which put the Treasury's finances in excellent shape.[280] I was indeed the "Man of the Hour," even if Abe Lincoln didn't think so.

I was also making progress in a pet project of mine to demonstrate to the world that freedmen were worthy of full enfranchisement and enlistment into the Union Army. To show that blacks were just as capable as whites to establish farming and conduct industry, I sponsored an experiment at Port Royal and the Sea Islands off the coast of South Carolina, which the Navy had managed to seize early in the war.

The fleeing white residents of Port Royal and the Sea Islands left behind large abandoned plantations and 10,000 black slaves. Northern charities, with my encouragement, stepped in to help the freed slaves establish self-sufficiency growing cotton and cultivating their own crops. Their sales of surplus crops and cotton allowed the freedmen to acquire capital to buy their own farms.[281]

Figure 53: Government Buildings for "Contrabands" on Hilton Head, South Carolina (PD)

My Treasury agents there assisted the Experiment by managing the abandoned plantations, collecting the valuable long-staple cotton grown there and craved by the New England cotton manufacturers, and training the black workers.[282] By March 1863, we were able to hold auctions for the sale of most of the land. Resident blacks were able to buy 2,000 acres. Some 16,000 acres, however, ended up in the hands of Northern speculators.[283]

- $ $ $ -

- $ -

The year 1863 proved to be a very favorable one, particularly on the battlefield, in the Treasury, and even in my personal life. Although the Union suffered a disastrous defeat at Chickamauga, in Tennessee, General Rosecrans' army was able to make a stand against Confederate General Braxton Bragg at Chattanooga. Railroads proved to be essential to that victory. In July came our victories at Gettysburg and Vicksburg.

I was able to report to Congress that the economy was producing over \$1 billion a year in revenue.[284] So pleased was I at the promising financial and military results that I had the good sense to grace newly-printed large denominations of Greenbacks with portraits of Lincoln, reserving my own for the smaller ones. It was sure to improve our political prospects with average citizens – particularly the more ubiquitous small denominations![285]

RUNNING THE "MACHINE".

Figure 54: "Running the Machine," political cartoon by John Cameron, 1864. Chase's successor as Treasury Secretary, William P. Fessenden, is "running" Chases "patented" Greenback machine. (PD)

But most importantly for me in that year was the marriage of my lovely daughter Kate to the wealthy New England industrialist and Rhode Island governor, William Sprague IV. Bill Sprague was a great supporter of my Port Royal and Sea Island Experiment. His family's textile empire in Rhode Island and Connecticut was instrumental in fostering the sale of cotton from the Sea Island plantations to its New England mills. He even recommended one of his associates, a former Rhode Island militia officer named William Reynolds, to act as my Treasury Agent to collect and ship the harvested cotton to the North.[286]

Figure 55: William and Kate Sprague, photo by Mathew Brady (PD)

Kate made a point of advancing my political career by making her mark in the Washington social world. She ran my household and held breakfasts for myself and a variety of Congressmen, military officers, bankers, and ministers. She even made it her duty to travel to military encampments to greet soldiers and officers on the battlefield. I even had Kate christen a revenue cutter that the Treasury Department had built and launched in New York.[287]

Figure 56: Kate Chase Sprague visiting Gen. J.J. Abercrombie at the battlefield defenses of Washington, D.C., circa 1863

I blessed the match of Kate and the now-Senator Sprague, and then set right to work to arrange a September wedding and reception in our home at Sixth and E Streets, N.E., on Capitol Hill. September is, after all, the best month for weather in Washington. Mother Nature provides messy snows, drenching rains, withering heat, and dreary clouds for eight months of the year. Then, she provides a gorgeous September of blue skies, cool evenings, and sunny days. After September, she messes it up again for the remainder of the year.

The wedding and reception were small but elegant affairs. About fifty of the most powerful personages in the capital and their wives were invited, including President Lincoln and his wife, Mary. He attended but she did not, ostensibly because she still mourned the recent death of her son, Willie. I had my suspicions, though, that in truth she was consumed with jealousy toward Kate. The wedding gifts that guests brought included the finest jewels, silver, and gold plate.[288]

- $ $ $ -

- $ -

Although all had been going so well for me personally at this time, my political world was collapsing in a disorganized heap.

Figure 57: Senator Samuel Pomeroy of Kansas (PD)

Much to my surprise, many political operatives that surrounded me were taking advantage of my ascending notoriety with the public and my financial successes at Treasury to advance their own political and financial agendas and to dispose of Lincoln as a Presidential candidate in 1864. A particularly vicious attack on Lincoln was authored by a committee headed by Senator Samuel Pomeroy of Kansas, ostensibly to advance my candidacy even though Pomeroy publicly avowed allegiance to Lincoln.

Pomeroy had a personal interest in a branch of the Kansas-Pacific Railroad then under construction, and he eagerly sought my Department's release of $640,000 under the Railroad Act of 1862 to reimburse him for his construction of forty miles of poorly-engineered track.[289] A "confidential" circular that the Senator distributed to several hundred of his "closest friends" in the press and Congress, entitled "The Next Presidential Election," excoriated Lincoln's handling of the Presidency. The circular accused Lincoln of being an indecisive, inept executive who jailed innocent civilians. It even compared Lincoln to Jefferson Davis and credited the latter for performing a better job of stewardship.[290]

The "Pomeroy Circular" did not mention me by name or endorse my candidacy for President, but its implications were clear to all. I was a favorite of the New York money-interests, railroad barons, and Radical Republicans. Lincoln was favored by more conservative New York political interests, who were controlled by William Seward and Thurlow Weed.

Pomeroy's own motive could not have been clearer – to curry favor with me by denigrating Lincoln and promoting me as an alternative, inducing me to release his railroad funds. The result was quite the opposite. The press reaction to the Circular was very unfavorable. I found myself being criticized even more fiercely and lost ground even in my home state of Ohio.[291]

I was mortified by the unexpected reaction and loss of support. Even more, the Circular sullied my good name once again in the eyes of Abe Lincoln. How much of this could the man take?

I wrote a letter to the President on February 22, 1864. I denied having anything to do with the Circular, but I had to admit that I had unwittingly consented that the Pomeroy committee could use my name (which it did not do). I concluded the letter with another offer to resign should I no longer merit the President's confidence. [292]

A few days later, the Republican conventions of Ohio and Indiana endorsed Lincoln for President in the 1864 election. Shortly thereafter, an obviously less-exasperated Lincoln wrote a reply to me, rejecting my resignation and noting his high regard for my financial prowess. He, asked me to remain in the Treasury.[293] I heaved a sigh of relief, but I also cursed my persistent stupidity over the double-edged sword of blandishment.

The financial situation declined as the price of gold soared over the value of Greenbacks, deflating the latter's value. My effort to prop up the value of Greenbacks by selling Treasury gold to depress its premium fell flat. Military movement seemed to be at a stalemate. Then a personnel flap unfolded at the New York Custom House – a patronage regime usually under my command and control – that seemed to get out of hand through corruption and larceny.

Thurlow Weed, the publisher of several New York newspapers and a powerful Republican politician, contacted Lincoln to have the corrupt officials excised from the Custom House. "Remove Barney and his four deputies as well who are intriguing against you," Weed told John Nicolay, whom Lincoln had sent to New York to speak with him. "Chase and Fremont are being talked of as presidential candidates," Weed also told him. "They might yet form and lead dangerous factions."[294]

Figure 58: Thurlow Weed (PD)

I made assiduous efforts to resolve the personnel matter, hoping to preserve my patronage control over the Custom House while doing no damage to my chances of winning the Republican nomination. These efforts failed. Yet once again, I found myself in the doghouse. I wrote another note to Lincoln acknowledging that my official relations with the President were now not the best, and if my continuation in my position was not "altogether agreeable to you," then I would again proffer my resignation.[295]

This time, the stupid thing that I did was to send the letter at all. It merely drew Lincoln's attention to myself as the probable culprit of a conspiracy in the Custom House to unseat him.

Lincoln exploded, suspecting my engaging in machinations to override his own patronage prerogatives. This time, he wrote out a terse note accepting my resignation. He handed another note to his secretary, John Hay, to present to the Senate.

"I wish you to be there when they meet," Lincoln told Hay when he gave him the second note. "It's a big fish. Mr. Chase has resigned and I have accepted his resignation. I thought I could not stand it any longer."[296]

PART FIVE
"CROSS OF GOLD"

———

Chapter Twenty-six – One Door Closes, Another Opens

———

I WAS SHOCKED, ABSOLUTELY SHOCKED, THAT President Lincoln had accepted my resignation.

I had offered my resignation several times before. I offered it whenever something went wrong and I was the culpable senior official. Each time, Abe seemed to be patient and forgiving with me. When the Pomeroy Circular hit, I offered it again but Lincoln rejected it, even praising me for good work. Surely that was a much more embarrassing imbroglio than the latest one.

So, when I offered my resignation yet again over the New York Custom House affair, I expected that the President would once again hedge his actions as he had done before. Apparently, however, I crossed a bright red political line this time – I interfered with Lincoln's absolute control over political patronage appointments in the Federal Government. That, among seasoned politicians, is *inexcusable*. And I, being one of that class, should have known better.

More likely, it was *Thurlow Weed's* control over New York Republican patronage that I had interfered with, not Lincoln's. Weed considered the New York Custom House to be within his bailiwick. I had already crossed *his* line by making many Treasury Agent appointments there without consulting him. Obviously, Lincoln owed him a lot and counted on his support for the Presidential nomination of 1864. Consequently, as Lincoln's nomination was gradually sewn up in state after state that spring and summer, it became evident to him that I was trouble and had to go.

Anxious for a long-delayed rest but uncertain about the future course of my political career, I resolved to calm my nerves with a tour of my beloved New England homestead during its always beautiful fall in that year of 1864.

- $ $ $ -

- $ -

When word of my resignation emerged on July 1, 1864, I was gratified to learn that money markets had plunged on the news. The value of gold in relation to Greenbacks had theretofore varied greatly on the New York markets with word of every Union victory or defeat. Prior to my resignation, a one-dollar gold coin was worth $1.15 in Greenbacks, a premium of merely 115 percent over face-value. Shortly after I resigned, however, the premium skyrocketed to *185 percent*. On July 2, it fell to 130 percent, and on July 11 it rose again to 184 percent. From thence to September 26, however, the price of gold fell to 87 percent, *below* par.[297] So it was clear that the gold coin premium over Greenbacks reacted to wartime calamities, and the markets obviously thought that my resignation was likewise such a calamity. But once the shock was gone, the premium disappeared and Greenbacks resumed their periodically volatile stability.

The presidential election campaign was by now well underway, and the path was clear for a Lincoln victory over his Democratic challenger, the hapless General McClellan. Lincoln steered a popular, conservative course toward emancipation of the slaves and reconstruction of the devastated South that comported with the preferences of his conservative supporters in the Cabinet, William Seward, Gideon Welles, and Montgomery Blair. Radical Republicans, who identified more with me but were bereft at this point of any other candidate to challenge Lincoln, preferred to punish the South. This view, however, did not sit well with Northerners who had family members there. McClellan, by contrast, spent much of his campaign time fighting with his own Democrats over their extreme peace plank that he vehemently opposed.

As I made my way to Boston, word came about General Sherman's burning of Atlanta and Admiral Farragut's capture of Mobile, Alabama, the last major port in Confederate hands. Lincoln's victory at the polls was now assured, and I now considered it expedient to patch things up with the President.

Traveling throughout New England, I stayed at the stately homes of several old friends. There were fishing trips, picnics, clam-bakes, and visits to historical sites.[298] I spent the end of my sojourn at my son-in-law Bill's sprawling farm on Narragansett Bay, near Newport, Rhode Island. There I joined Kate and my younger daughter, Nettie, for long walks along the Bay and games of croquet.[299]

One sad thing became very disturbing – the apparent collapse of my daughter Kate's marriage to Bill. It drifted rapidly toward the rocks. Kate had hoped that Bill would take her on a trip to Europe, but that didn't happen. Instead, Kate became pregnant, which did not improve her mood. Bill had also resumed drinking, not excessively but somewhat immoderately for her tastes. Kate, Nettie, and I had several long, tearful walks along the Bay in which I tried to console and advise her.

Figure 59: Nettie, Salmon, and Kate Chase

- $ $ $ -

- $ -

Roger B. Taney, our eighty-six- year-old Chief Justice of the United States Supreme Court for over 30 years, was in failing health. President Lincoln and many others detested him, particularly for his disastrous *Dred Scott* decision that truly impelled the Civil War. He was a persistent thorn in Lincoln's side when the President felt the need to jail traitorous Confederates. Lincoln denied them the right to file writs of *habeas corpus* to have a court determine if they were jailed unjustly. But Taney would simply overrule the President. It certainly appeared strange to me that Taney would see fit to grant traitors a right otherwise afforded only to loyal American citizens.

Taney's Southern sympathies, matched by nearly half of the Supreme Court in the early stages of the war, induced the Radical Republicans in Congress to enact a law to "pack" the Supreme Court with an extra seat to break the tie. In May of 1863, Lincoln chose California Supreme Court Chief Justice Stephen Johnson Field, a Union Democrat, to fill it.

Mercifully, about a year later, Taney died.

Along with myself, there were many potential candidates for Lincoln's choice of a new Chief – Edwin Stanton, Montgomery Blair, Associate Justice Noah Swayne of Ohio, and a well-known lawyer from New York named William M. Evarts.[300] These gentlemen were popular with the conservative Republican wing of Seward and Weed, whereas I endeared myself more with the Radical Republicans.

Lincoln absolutely jumped at the opportunity to get me out of his way as a serious contender for the Republican Presidential nomination. Taney died on the very day that I was making a stump speech for the Republicans in Covington, Kentucky, just across the Ohio River from Cincinnati. That apparently convinced him that he could sell me to skeptical conservative Senators as a party friend on the Court.

As the Second Session of the Thirty-eighth Congress convened on December 5, 1864, I hurried back to Washington from my travels to see what might develop. Upon my arrival, I learned that the President had placed my name in nomination for the Chief Justiceship on the second day of the session and the Senate had confirmed me unanimously that same day.[301] Two weeks later, I was sworn in as the Sixth Chief Justice.

Despite my longstanding presidential ambitions, I cannot say that I was displeased with this appointment. Every lawyer in the country desires to be a Supreme Court Justice, and even more, the Chief Justice. It's a lifetime job. One need no longer seek out and satisfy finicky clients who may drop you as their counsel at any moment. Not only that, one is empowered to *do justice*, not to just represent one side of a dispute. In cases, no side has the moral high ground – each side is always as guilty as the other of *something*. In representing his client zealously, a lawyer must sell some part of his soul to the Devil in order to make arguments that gloss over a client's bad acts. Justices do not have this problem.

- $ $ $ -

- $ -

Initially I presided over a ten-Justice Court. However, Justice John Catron died within five months of my arrival. His death followed by one month the shocking and horrendous assassination of President Lincoln by a Confederate sympathizer as he attended a play at Ford's Theater in Washington. He was succeeded by his Vice-President, a Union Democrat named Andrew Johnson.

The majority-Republican Congress did not want a Democrat to choose the next Supreme Court Justice. So, in 1866, it passed, and President Johnson apparently unwittingly signed, a Judiciary Act abolishing Catron's seat.[302] Hence, we were pared down to nine Justices. They are portrayed in the 1867 photograph below – myself in the middle as Chief, and seated on either side of me from left to right, Associate Justices David Davis, Noah Swayne, Robert Grier, James Wayne, Samuel Nelson, Nathan Clifford, Samuel Miller, and Stephen Field.

Figure 60: Chief Justice Chase's Supreme Court, February 1867 (PD)

Chapter Twenty-seven – Greenbacks Return to Haunt Me

———

THE WAR WAS OVER, BUT GREENBACKS WERE NOT. During the war, the face-value of the $450 million worth of Greenbacks of various denominations that the Treasury had issued under the authority of the wartime First, Second, and Third Legal Tender Acts had dropped in relation to the equivalent face-value of gold coin. Gold fetched a premium over Greenbacks of as much as 158 percent in July 1864 (corresponding, of course, with the financial shock that accompanied my resignation as Secretary of the Treasury). By the time of General Lee's surrender to General Grant at Appomattox Courthouse in April 1865, however, the Greenback had recovered its value to only 150 Greenback dollars to every 100 dollars in gold.[303]

Greenbacks that were not redeemable in gold or silver continued to be used as our domestic currency long after the war. The states of California and Oregon never accepted them as legal tender and would not accept them in payment of taxes, primarily because gold and silver coin were plentiful there.[304] The courts of fifteen other states upheld the constitutionality of Greenbacks, but the court of Kentucky did not.[305]

Nevertheless, Greenbacks remained at remarkably manageable premiums for the duration of the war except for its last year, and were instrumental in expanding the supply of money in the Northern economy to fund the war's enormous expense for labor, supplies, and soldiers. United States Notes have since then become an accepted form of currency that no longer depends on an ever-varying supply of gold or the uncertain solvency of private banks that issue their own demand notes.

- $ $ $ -

- $ -

Despite my enormous sense of satisfaction at having solved a thorny national financial problem in a way that was instrumental to achieving my long-sought dreams of ending slavery in the United States and winning the war, I was well-aware of a festering legal problem with Greenbacks, especially now that I occupied the highest judicial office in the land.

Nowhere in the Constitution does it say that the Federal Government may print paper money. It says nothing about paper money at all. It provides Congress only with the power "[t]o *coin* Money, [and] regulate the Value thereof ...."[306] To "*coin*" a metal into money is not understood in the lexicon of finance to be the same as to "*print*" money on paper. As for the states, the Constitution explicitly forbids them to coin money at all, or to "make any Thing but gold and silver Coin a Tender in Payment of Debts ...."[307]

This preference for gold and silver coin in the Constitution is there for a reason. During the Revolutionary War, the Continental Congress printed dollars that were to be redeemed in silver after the war. The value of these "Continentals," as they were then called, was not respected by American merchants. "Not worth a Continental" was a by-word for valuelessness among the populace because of the ease with which the British could make counterfeits, the unwillingness of the states to pay their fair share of the costs of the Continental Congress to prosecute the war, and the perceived unlikelihood that the Continental Congress would ever have enough gold or silver to redeem its notes.[308]

James Madison, in *The Federalist Papers* that he composed with Alexander Hamilton and John Jay, made note of the odiousness of paper money that had been issued by the states during the Revolution, and hailed the Constitution's banning of it in the future:

> *The loss which America has sustained since the peace, from the pestilent effects of paper money on the necessary confidence between man and man, on the necessary confidence in the public councils, on the industry and morals of the people, and on the character of republican government, constitutes an enormous debt against the States chargeable with this unadvised measure, which must long remain unsatisfied; or rather an accumulation of guilt, which can be expiated no otherwise than by a voluntary sacrifice on the altar of justice of the power which has been the instrument of it. In addition to these persuasive considerations, it may be observed that the same reasons which show the necessity of denying to the States the power of regulating coin prove with equal force that they ought not to be at liberty to substitute a paper medium in the place of coin.*[309]

These sentiments of the Founding Fathers have long guided me. It was the reason why, despite my recognition of the expediency of issuing Greenbacks during the height of the war for the purpose of securing our military needs against a powerful enemy, I had always expressed my strongest reservations about our reliance on anything but gold and silver coin as legal tender for all debts, public and private.

Soon after my appointment to the Court as its Chief Justice, I came face-to-face with James Madison's farsighted warning.

- $ $ $ -

- $ -

On June 20, 1860, a certain Mrs. Hepburn signed a promissory note to pay one Henry Griswold the sum of $11,250 on February 20, 1862. At that time, all contracts for the payment of money were universally and legally understood to be for payment in coin unless expressly stipulated otherwise.[310]

Five days after the due date of the note, on February 25, 1862, Congress passed the First Legal Tender Act authorizing the issuance of United States Notes – that is, Greenbacks. The Act provided that such notes shall "be lawful money and a legal tender in payment of all debts, public and private, within the United States" except for duties on imports and interest payments on bank notes.[311]

Mrs. Hepburn did not pay the note on time, and in March 1864 Mr. Griswold sued for payment on the note, plus interest, in the Louisville, Kentucky Chancery Court. Mrs. Hepburn, as the defendant, paid into the Court Greenbacks in the face-value amount of $12,720, the amount of the note plus interest and costs accrued by the date of payment. Mr. Griswold refused to accept the Greenbacks as payment, but the Chancery Court, "resolving all doubts in favor of the Congress," declared the tender good and adjudged the debt, interest, and costs to have been satisfied.[312]

Mr. Griswold appealed to the Court of Errors of Kentucky, and that Court reversed the judgment and remanded the case to the Chancery Court with instructions to enter a contrary judgment that favored Mr. Griswold. Mrs. Hepburn appealed that ruling to the U.S. Supreme Court.[313]

By their own express terms, the Legal Tender Acts of 1862 and 1863 make Greenbacks legal tender in payment of debts, public and private, that are contracted *before* as well as *after* their dates of enactment. Accordingly, the statutes validated Mrs. Hepburn's tender of Greenbacks in payment of the note, interest, and costs accrued, and the Court of Chancery had so held.

Before we received this case, our Supreme Court had already determined, in a few cases the year before, that neither taxes imposed by state legislation nor demands upon contracts which require in writing for payment in coin or bullion are included by legislative intent within the meaning of "all debts, public and private," in the Legal Tender Acts.[314] This new case, however, was the first instance in which we were asked whether that term can constitutionally embrace debts that are neither in payment of taxes nor required by contract to be paid in specie. Moreover, we were asked whether such debts "contracted before as well as after the date of the act" could be paid for in Greenbacks.[315]

As I have already said, I have always been a "hard money" man. I have always believed that gold and silver coin are the only lawful currencies that should be allowed in commerce because they possess intrinsic value that is recognized by all. I had issued reports to Congress during my term in the Cabinet saying as much.

During the war, however, I was beset as Secretary of the Treasury by the fact that there was simply not enough gold and silver coin in the land that we could get our hands on to pay the enormous expenses that we faced in wartime. Even though we issued hundreds of millions of dollars in bonds and demand notes to borrow the needed funds; and even though we raised tariffs on every conceivable import; and even though we had invented an entirely new "income tax" that would seize a part of the very earnings of every man in America that he had made to feed, house, and clothe his family; it still wasn't enough to pay for the enormous cost of salaries for millions of soldiers, wooden and ironclad warships, cannon, mortars, rifles, railroads, horses, caissons, and tents that were desperately needed to fight a formidable foe, equally matched to us and frightfully effective, for five long years in the bloodiest of wars.

I had lengthy arguments on this case with my colleagues on the Court in our conferences. Six others beside me were "hard money" men as well – Associate Justices Grier, Wayne, Nelson, Clifford, and Field. But three – Associate Justices Miller, Swayne, and Davis – favored "soft money" and vehemently disagreed.

Sam Miller and I got into a rather heated exchange in our early January conference, after our first "straw poll" indicated that the hard-money view would prevail.

Figure 61: Chief Justice Chase

Figure 62: Associate Justice Miller

"Chief," said Sam, "I am having a very hard time accepting your position on this *Hepburn* case. Of all the men here, I would have thought you would be willing to uphold the Legal Tender Acts. Nothing in the Constitution precludes Congress from making United States Notes legal tender for debts predating the acts, and the 'Necessary and Proper' Clause of the Constitution clearly broadens the power of Congress to take whatever steps were necessary to prosecute the war. It was you who, as Secretary of the Treasury, advocated for them and put them into effect, with excellent results."

"Brother Sam," I replied, "I had no other choice at the time but to do that. There was not enough gold or silver in the land to prosecute the war in 1862, so a substitute had to be created to meet the exigency. We did many things like that in Lincoln's Cabinet. We frequently stretched the Constitution beyond its boundaries under the authority of the President as Commander-in-Chief. Lincoln himself suspended the writ of *habeas corpus* without Congress' consent, which roiled Congress and the courts for years afterward.

"We were in no position to use the Constitution to tie Lincoln's hands when the rebellion was very much alive, and the very life of the Constitution was at stake," I told him. "Now that is no longer the case, and admittedly with the benefit of hindsight, I truly believe that it was unconstitutional for us – for *me*—to do so."

"Every sovereign country on the face of the Earth has the power to declare its paper money to be legal tender," Miller replied. "You will be leaving out our country alone, and its life may depend on it, as it did in the last war!"

"I realize that in extraordinary times, such measures have to be taken," I told Miller. "But we are no longer in extraordinary times, and this is not a case about extraordinary times. This is not a debt for war materiel. This is a simple promissory note, made before the war, with the parties' full expectation at that time that it would be repaid in specie. After all, the money that was *lent* in the first place was specie. How could Mrs. Hepburn cheat Mr. Griswold out of the full value of his loan by handing him depreciated money, even if it is declared on the face of it to be at par value?"

"The Legal Tender Acts are unconstitutional *ex post facto* laws!" someone growled further down the long conference table. We turned to see who it was. It was Justice Stephen Field, our new colleague from the "Wild West" of California.

Figure 63: Associate Justice Stephen Johnson Field

Justice Field spoke on this topic with considerable authority. He wrote the majority opinions in *Cummings v. Missouri* and *Ex parte Garland* in 1866, in which Miller and I both dissented.[316] In those cases, so-called "loyalty oaths" that certain states required persons seeking certain positions to swear after the war, attesting that they had never supported the Rebellion in any way, were deemed by Justice Field's majority opinion to be unconstitutional "*ex post facto*" laws, wrongfully punishing conduct that was not illegal when it was committed.[317]

"Are you saying," Miller turned to Field, with a puzzled look, "that Congress cannot pass a law that makes legal something that was heretofore illegal? It is my understanding, Brother Field, that the *ex post facto* principle works the other way around. Congress cannot pass a law that makes *illegal* something that was heretofore *legal.*"

"Not when you take Gresham's Law into account!" Field snapped back. "It's one of the oldest rules in classical economics! 'Bad money drives out good money!' Legalize paper money, and pretty soon all gold and silver coin disappears. Effectively, they become illegal! No one receives back as repayment in kind that which they lent! Their loans are discounted in value immediately. And so, it is an *ex post facto* law—gold and silver coin, which was legal tender when the deal was struck, is now made illegal by *fiat*!"

Field's argument made a great deal of sense to me. Gresham's economic principle was well-recognized and indeed worked as he described. Creating a paper money substitute for gold and silver coin effectively led to the hoarding of such coins, and only paper money was left to circulate among the public. It would effectively devalue the currency. A lender would not be repaid the value he originally lent.

"I accept Gresham's Law, Brother Field," Miller replied. "But Gresham's Law adds only one factor to the question that you overstate – it adds a 'premium' to the exchange of gold and silver for Greenbacks. It creates a market between the two types of currency. You can use one or the other to pay debts, simply by taking the premium into account with the transaction. But the transaction *itself* does not change. An apple is still exchanged for an orange, using the standard unit of value for whatever currency is available to make it happen – in our case, dollars."

"And the premium thus adds to the cost of the orange?" I asked Miller rhetorically. "It seems to me that the price has changed," I added.

"Typically, Chief, a financial clearinghouse is not readily available at every grocery market," Miller replied with a smile. "It is not the case that the paper money used in the transaction must be immediately transformed into gold on the spot. More often, the paper money is pocketed by the seller and used some time later to buy something else, like a potato or something. There is no exchange of paper for gold or silver coin there either. The point is that an economic transfer is made using a currency's standard unit of value, and so, a dollar in payment given begets a dollar in good or service received."

Sam Miller's argument was a cogent one, a sophisticated one, and was borne out by the very experience that we had gone through in the late war. The Northern economy did not die with the advent of Greenbacks, as the Southern economy did with long-term unfulfilled promises of repayment in gold. Instead, it thrived and grew to serve the needs of the war effort just when we needed it. There did indeed seem to be some kind of science to it.

"Gentlemen, if you will allow me," I interjected now, eager to move on to other pressing matters. "I will prepare a draft in line with the straw poll that we have just taken, and circulate it for comment and dissent. We will discuss the result at the next conference in two weeks. Brother Sam, I trust that you will draft a dissenting opinion."

"I certainly will, Chief," Sam replied.

- $ $ $ -

- $ -

The essential matter that I faced in this draft was whether the Legal Tender Acts could constitutionally make Greenbacks legal tender for all debts, public and private, that had arisen *before* the Acts were passed. No one questioned that they could be for debts incurred *after* their passage.

We had already decided in earlier cases that contracts made before the passage of the Acts that expressly required repayment in specie had to be paid for in specie. We had also concluded that certain state tax payments had to be made in specie rather than in Greenbacks. [318] In this case, by contrast, the contract at issue did not provide for the type of currency to be used for payment, and it was not for payment of a state tax.

No provision of the Constitution forbids the Federal Government in express terms from printing money. No provision authorizes it either. This power, if it exists at all, could only come from the clause for "implied powers" that are made available to the Federal Government, which is known as the "Necessary and Proper Clause."

The Necessary and Proper Clause grants the Federal Government "power to make all laws necessary and proper for carrying into execution the powers expressly granted to Congress or vested by the Constitution in the government or in any of its departments or officers."[319]

The nation's first Chief Justice, John Marshall, provided a cogent and well-recognized explanation for when the Necessary and Proper Clause can be called upon. He held for a unanimous Court in the landmark case of *McCullough v. Maryland*:

> *Let the end be legitimate, let it be within the scope of the Constitution, and all means which are appropriate, which are plainly adapted to that end, which are not prohibited, but consistent with the letter and spirit of the Constitution, are constitutional.*[320]

Marshall further explained in that case that where Congress passes laws for the accomplishment of objects not entrusted to it, those laws fall outside of the scope of the Necessary and Proper Clause and are unconstitutional. Where, on the other hand, there is no Constitutional prohibition of the law and the law is calculated to effect any of the objects entrusted to the government, then it is within Constitutional bounds under the Necessary and Proper Clause.[321]

My judicial compass, then, pointed to the objectives of the Federal Government's expressly "entrusted powers" to find, if I could, those which justify it to print paper currency instead of relying exclusively on gold and silver coin.

I certainly could not find such justification in the express power of Congress to coin money.[322] It, simply, is not the same thing. Nor could I find such justification in Congress' express power to regulate the value of coined money in the United States, or of foreign coins. [323] To "regulate" such value is to determine the weight, purity, form, impression, and denomination of coins and their relationships to each other in connection with the monetary unit of the United States. One cannot determine such things in connection with mere paper.

I did not find such justification in the power of Congress to issue bills of credit.[324] This power of the old Congress of the Confederation was extended to Congress under the new Constitution, but it was expressly held by this Court that such power did not include the authority to declare such bills and notes to be legal tender. They were simply written evidence that the government owed a debt.

I turned, then, from those express powers that Congress had over money generally to those express powers that prompted Congress to pass these Legal Tender Acts in the first place – the power to conduct war, to regulate commerce, and to borrow money. These were the most relevant powers to me personally, as they were the ones that I relied upon in implementing the Legal Tender Acts while I was Secretary of the Treasury.

Congress has the power to declare war. Hence, it has the power to carry on that war by issuing bills of credit and circulating notes in discharge of government obligations. It facilitates the use of such notes to make them legal tender in payment of existing debts, so the argument goes. Ergo, the Legal Tender Acts are constitutionally implied powers out of the power to wage war.

I could find nothing in my personal beliefs and learning on which I could accept this logic on its face. It is an implied power to print money solely out of the *need* for that money in order to accomplish something. Everything requires money. Every state power requires money. It is required to build bridges and post roads, to build government buildings, to pay government employees. If all that is needed for the purpose of creating money is to have a *need* for it, then does it have any *intrinsic value* in and of itself?

I found this argument to carry the doctrine of implied powers very far beyond any extent hitherto given to it. I believe most fundamentally that money is a thing of intrinsic value, and that its usefulness in carrying on commerce is that it can be used to value products and services in relation to one another by reference to its own intrinsic value. If this intrinsic value is not necessary to the existence of money itself, then *any* means which promotes an end within the scope of a general power, whether "appropriate" or not, may be done in the exercise of an implied power. But how can one imply power to a valueless thing?

It is also argued that the relation of an implied power to expressly delegated powers is not this Court's concern. It is for Congress alone to discern. But to allow Congress to decide this question exclusively would convert the government, which the people ordained as a government of limited powers, into a government of unlimited powers. It would obviate this Court's duty to determine what is constitutional and what is unconstitutional.

We must decide, then, whether Congress' express power to conduct war, and its express power to issue notes in payment thereof, imply a power to make such notes legal tender? While I was Treasury Secretary, I did not think that the quality of United States Notes as legal tender added any attribute to their ready circulation as currency. To me, it was *the fact that the Notes were accepted by the government as payment for dues owed to it* that bolstered their acceptability. A seller of a good or service, in my view, accepts a United States Note as payment because he can then use the Note to pay his federal income tax by that exact amount. Everyone wants to be able to do that, so everyone accepts the United States Note as payment in the amount of its face value. That there is a law decreeing that the Note is "legal tender" adds nothing to the Note's usefulness.

History in times of war shows that when the large costs of war are met by government notes, they circulate most readily and suffer little, if any, depreciation. The provision in the Acts making the notes legal tender was, indeed, an afterthought; it was their availability to pay taxes and duties that made them useful for the war effort.

My five concurring colleagues and I could see no gain to compelling creditors to receive Greenbacks in satisfaction of pre-existing debts. The government certainly could not obtain better terms for goods and services with them, nor could it shield prices from inflation. By contrast, whatever benefit was perceived to making them legal tender was outweighed by the losses of property, the increased fluctuation of currency and values, increased inflation, and the long train of evils that we learned from the Revolutionary period flow from the use of irredeemable paper money. The implied power to make paper money legal tender, then, did not impress us as this was the sort of expedient that was appropriate and plainly adapted for executing the power to declare and carry on war.

- $ $ $ -

- $ -

Throughout January of 1870, Justice Grier was in very bad health. He had suffered three strokes in the last three years, and it looked as if this month would be his last. He remained on the Court through January, however, and made up one of my supporting colleagues on *Hepburn*.

Figure 64: Associate Justice Robert C. Grier (PD)

I completed the remainder of my draft, touching upon a few more points, and circulated it to my brethren as promised for their review, comment, concurrence, and dissent in time for the next conference.

Sam Miller, of course, was the first one to approach me. Justices Swayne and Davis joined him in support. Justice Miller preceded me on the Court, having been appointed by President Lincoln in 1862. He was a former Whig, a present Republican, an abolitionist, and a Unitarian. He hailed from Keokuk, Iowa, and had practiced medicine before teaching himself law. Sam Miller was a brilliant man and a prolific opinion-writer, and his views carried great weight among our colleagues.

After concluding my usual opening remarks at the conference, Sam spoke up. "Chief, I have read your draft and discussed it with some colleagues here. It surprised me, I must say, because given your background at Treasury I would have expected you to support the Legal Tender Acts to the fullest.

"First," Sam said, "there are several things on which we all agree. The power to declare paper money to be legal tender is not an express power explicitly set forth in the Constitution, but may be an implied power under the Necessary and Proper Clause of the Constitution. Nothing in the Constitution expressly forbids Congress to exercise this power. By contrast, the states are expressly forbidden to declare anything but gold and silver coin to be legal tender. So, we all agree, if this implied power rests with any government entity at all, it rests with the Federal Government and no other.

"We diverge from there," he continued. "To say it loosely, Chief, the Necessary and Proper Clause means two entirely different things to the two of us and our supporting brethren. To us, it is an *expansive* provision, which allows the Federal Government to exercise Constitutionally unstated powers when to do so is in furtherance of its express powers. To you, it is a *restrictive* provision, which permits unstated powers to be exercised only when it is clearly demonstrated that doing so is *absolutely necessary* to carry out the exercise of express powers.

"Now also, Chief," Sam continued, "we differ on how an implied power can accomplish an expressly-defined end. We say that *any* means that is available to Congress to exercise an implied power is acceptable, so long that it is in keeping with the letter and spirit of the Constitution. You, by contrast, say that *only an absolutely necessary means, and no other*, is available to Congress to carry out the implied power.

"I think that those of us who agree with me can accept everything that you've said so far, Sam," I interjected, turning to my colleagues who nodded their assent.

"Fine," said Sam with a smile. He then leaned forward over the conference table. "Then where we disagree fundamentally, Chief," he said slowly, "is over *what money is.*"

It had not occurred to me until Sam said this that there was even an open question as to what money was. "Well, the Constitution is very clear on that point, Sam," I replied. "It is gold or silver coin. Nothing more."

"The Constitution *prohibits* the states from declaring anything but gold and silver coin to be legal tender, Chief," Sam answered, "but it does not *affirmatively state* what is *within the universe* of all that is 'legal tender.' That is left undefined, and that is where Congress' lawmaking power comes in and where the Necessary and Proper Clause operates."

"It cannot possibly mean that," I replied. "If the Constitution were so open-ended, then Congress could vote tomorrow to declare that corn cobs are 'legal tender for all debts public and private.' That implies that Congress can do anything, and it is beyond dispute that the Constitution was designed to *limit* the powers of Congress to doing only certain express things, not to open the door to doing anything."

"As I said, Chief," Sam replied, "that is where the Necessary and Proper Clause comes in. The open end is not unrestrained; it is limited to what Chief Justice Marshall said it was – 'Let the end be legitimate, let it be within the scope of the Constitution, and all means which are appropriate, which are plainly adapted to that end, which are not prohibited, but consistent with the letter and spirit of the Constitution, are constitutional.' The key words are a 'legitimate end,' 'within the scope of the Constitution,' and 'consistent with the letter and spirit of the Constitution.'"

I pondered this view for a minute or two. There was absolute silence in the room. At last, I said, "Sam, come back for a moment to what you said earlier about our difference being as to what money is. What do you mean by that?"

"I apologize in advance, Chief," Sam said, "if what I am about to say appears to you to be somewhat presumptuous of what your interpretation of money is. But having said that, allow me to draw the distinction for you as I see it.

"You say that money is gold and silver coin. They are metals, with a certain weight, consistency, and definition. They are malleable into coin with government-sanctioned figures impressed upon them and a denomination in dollars noted on them for what they are worth. You view money as that metal object itself that is generally called 'money.'

"I say that 'money' is *not a metal object*. It is a *concept*; an *idea*. It is a unit of exchange for goods and services. It is not the metal itself that is the 'money;' it is the *value that is assigned to it* that is the 'money.'

Its use is to compare the relative value of goods and services to one another and to allow buyers and sellers to purchase them for value given and received. It is what permits goods and services to change hands without requiring a duel, so to speak.

"Now, if we view gold and silver coin as money, we do so because mankind has done so from time immemorial. But he can also do so *by law*. If the law of the land states that a piece of paper with a fancy design on it to deter counterfeiting and a picture of Salmon P. Chase in the corner is 'legal tender for all debts, public and private,' well, then, it *is* that. And the value of that money, like the value of gold and silver coin, is that the seller who accepts that money as payment for goods and services rendered recognizes that he can turn around and buy goods and services with it from someone else, for the exact value stated on the money.

"That, in a nutshell, Chief," Sam concluded, "is all that money is."

I pondered this explanation for another couple of minutes. There was, again, a dead silence in the room. I then said, "Gentlemen, I think that now is a good time for us to stretch our legs and take a short recess of about one-half hour." We all stood up together and filed out of the room to various corners of the U.S. Capitol Building.

- $ $ $ -

- $ -

"What do you make of this, Stephen?" I asked Justice Field as we filed out of the Men's Room and stood in the hall to smoke our cigars.

"Well, like you, Chief, I cannot get out of my head the notion that you cannot buy something with nothing. You cannot buy a diamond ring with a piece of paper that says 'this note is legal tender for all debts, public and private,' and that's all there is to it. You must give the seller *something of value* in order to get *something of value* in return. The whole notion of a 'transaction' is an exchange of *things of value*.

"Look at the facts of the case, Chief," Stephen continued. "Griswold had a visceral reaction when Hepburn paid him in paper dollars for the gold he had lent to her. He felt as if he had been cheated. There is a premium that must be paid to obtain payment in gold rather than paper. That is Griswold's proprietary loss."

"That is precisely the problem that I'm having, Stephen," I replied. "I think that Sam Miller is reading too much into the 'Necessary and Proper' Clause. The Federal Government is a government of *limited* powers, and the Necessary and Proper Clause is meant to extend the express powers only as far as is needed to implement them.

"So, for example," I continued, "where the Constitution gives Congress the power 'to establish Post Offices and post Roads,' then it is implicitly empowered to buy brick and mortar to build the buildings and macadam to pave the roads. But it is not implicitly empowered to build railroads and railway stations!"

"That's it exactly, Chief," said Stephen. "This country is devoted to private enterprise. The government is not supposed to interfere with private enterprise. It is private enterprise that advances the country, such as to build railroads and railway stations. The government is limited to running a post office. If the country wants the government to build railroads, it must amend the Constitution to allow it."

We seemed to be of like minds. "What do you think of Sam's notion that money is merely a unit of exchange, not some specific thing of value?"

Stephen pulled a long draw from his cigar, then blew out a perfect smoke ring. "Something for nothing," he replied contemptuously.

- $ $ $ -

- $ -

At our next judicial conference, Stephen and I relayed to Sam Miller the gist of the conversation that we had.

Miller smiled and shook his head slightly.

"Gentlemen," he said, "permit me to enlighten you on what, to my way of thinking, took place at your conversation in front of the Men's Room.

"You posited two entirely separate forms of currency," he said. "One is a currency based on the weight of a certain amount of gold. The other is a currency based on the denomination in dollars that is written on a piece of paper, together with a statement on the paper that 'this note is legal tender for all debts, public and private,' in that denomination.

"Someone else has in his possession an apple that both of you want. One of you is willing to give that person half an ounce of gold in return for the apple. The other is willing to give that person a United States Note denominated as 'One Dollar.' Let's say that the holder of the apple accepts the paper bill in payment for the apple.

"That apple-seller has no need whatsoever for the gold that the other potential purchaser has. He has received his consideration for giving up the apple, because he knows that he is able to pass that piece of paper on to someone else who is willing to sell him something for one dollar that he wants later.

"Now suppose the former holder offers the One Dollar bill to the gold holder and the latter refuses it. He feels that his gold is worth more than One Dollar. Well, one of two things will happen – either there will be no transaction, or the gold holder will accept the bill in return for a smaller portion of the gold.

"Now all that you have done, Gentlemen," Miller concluded, "is to set a price for the gold in terms of the paper currency. *Both may be used in the future to settle debts with others.* One can do so because tradition wills it to be so; the other can do so because the law wills it to be so.

"So can you truthfully say, sirs," he said to Stephen and me, "that there is value only in one of these objects but not in the other?"

"I would say so, Sam," Stephen Field retorted. "Gold has been recognized through the ages, among all civilizations, as a thing of value. It has been universally held to be able to convey possession of nearly anything from one person to another, depending on its amount. But a paper One Dollar bill, Sam, is a creature of a government, something which people may or may not recognize; something which people on this side of the Atlantic Ocean may recognize but people on the other side may not. That, to me, does not constitute money."

"But you recognize, Stephen," Sam replied, "that on this side of the Atlantic, where the United States government is the supreme ruler of the land, all recognize its laws and accept its lawful currency as money. True?"

"All *law-abiding* persons do, Sam," Stephen answered. "Robbers will only accept gold. Offer that man a paper dollar instead of a sack of gold, and you may very well lose your life."

We all knew that Stephen Field, a lawyer from the Wild West, was speaking from experience.

- $ $ $ -

- $ -

Hepburn v. Griswold consumed much of the Justices' time during the remainder of our 1868 term. On November 27, 1869, we decided the case in conference just before the beginning of our new December term.[325] We remained not of one mind on it.

On February 7, 1870, we issued the Court's decision.[326] It was a six-to-three decision; the Opinion of the Court was written by myself on behalf of six Justices, and a dissent was written by Justice Miller on behalf of the other three. I read the majority opinion in open Court.

In my reading of the Opinion, I first laid out the distinction between the two forms of currency:

> *[Paper] currency ... consists of notes or promises to pay impressed upon paper, prepared in convenient form for circulation and protected against counterfeiting by suitable devices and penalties. [Gold and silver coin] possess intrinsic value determined by the weight and fineness of the metal; [paper currency has] no intrinsic value, but a purchasing value, determined by the quantity in circulation, by general consent to its currency in payments, and by opinion as to the probability of redemption in coin.*[327]

I also set forth two well-known economic laws of currency that set paper money apart from coin:

There is a well-known law of currency that notes or promises to pay, unless made conveniently and promptly convertible into coin at the will of the holder, can never, except under unusual and abnormal conditions, be at par in circulation with coin. It is an equally well-known law that depreciation of notes must increase with the increase of the quantity put in circulation and the diminution of confidence in the ability or disposition to redeem. Their appreciation follows the reversal of these conditions. No act making them a legal tender can change materially the operation of these laws. [328]

I conceded that it was the express intention of Congress in the Legal Tender Acts "to make the notes authorized by it a legal tender in payment of debts contracted before the passage of the act."[329]

We were squarely faced, therefore, with the question of whether Congress had the power so to do. We could find no authority in the Constitution to do it, except as an implied power under the Necessary and Proper Clause, if at all.[330]

We all agreed that the relevant rule of construction of this clause of the Constitution was as stated by Chief Justice Marshall in *McCullough v. Maryland*: "*Let the end be legitimate, let it be within the scope of the Constitution, and all means which are appropriate, which are plainly adapted to that end, which are not prohibited, but consistent with the letter and spirit of the Constitution, are constitutional.*"[331] This rule, I explained, refers to "*laws, not absolutely necessary indeed, but appropriate, plainly adapted to constitutional and legitimate ends; laws not prohibited, but consistent with the letter and spirit of the Constitution; laws really calculated to effect objects entrusted to the government.*"[332]

The power to make paper currency legal tender, I held, "is certainly not the same power as the power to coin money."[333] That power, rather, is only "a power to determine the weight, purity, form, impression, and denomination of the several coins and their relation to each other, and the relations of foreign coins to the monetary unit of the United States."[334] Nor was it a power possessed by the old Congress of the Confederation that passed into the Congress of the Constitution.[335]

Was it, then, "a means appropriate and plainly adapted to the execution of the power to carry on war, the power to regulate commerce, and of the power to borrow money?" To the war power, I expressed my doubts. "Is there," I asked rhetorically, "any power which does not involve the use of money?" This argument, I felt, "prove[s] too much." It pushes "the doctrine of implied powers very far beyond any extent hitherto given to it." It suggests that anything which "in any degree promotes an end within the scope of a general power, whether, in the correct sense of the word, appropriate or not, may be done in the exercise of an implied power."[336] I could not buy into this notion. Nor could I accept that only Congress and not the courts should answer this question exclusively. To allow that "would convert the government, which the people ordained as a government of limited powers, into a government of unlimited powers."[337]

The question reduced, then, to the specific issue of whether Congress had the power to declare paper currency to be a legal tender in payment of debts that came into being before the acts were passed. [338] In my Opinion for the Court, I disagreed that this aspect of paper currency even mattered to its value in circulation. Notes that were not declared to be legal tender circulated as well, and were not discounted by reason of their not having been declared legal tender.

The most useful aspect of the legal tender notes, I said, was their ability to pay government dues. This aspect enhanced their demand and increased their circulation in an era of high taxes, large loans, and heavy government disbursements in wartime. Eminent writers denied that the quality of being legal tender adds anything at all to the credit or usefulness of government notes.[339]

I went on at some length thereafter about how little the government gets out of making such notes legal tender. It cannot obtain new supplies or services at a cheaper rate than for gold, because no one will take such notes for more than they are worth at the time of a new contract. They depreciate like any other form of payment, and if such notes are excessive in amount, depreciation will be aggravated. Designating such notes as legal tender adds nothing of value to them in this regard.[340]

Most importantly, I held that compelling individuals to accept such notes as legal tender for pre-existing debts owed to them is outweighed "by the losses of property, the derangement of business, the fluctuations of currency and values, and the increase of prices to the people and the government, and the long train of evils which flow from the use of irredeemable paper money."[341]

In sum, I concluded that making mere promises to pay dollars as legal tender in payment of debts previously contracted is not "an appropriate and plainly adapted means for the execution of the power to declare and carry on war."[342] Nor could I find that making bills of credit legal tender is "consistent with the spirit of the Constitution" because it interferes with private contracts.[343]

"[W]e cannot doubt that a law not made in pursuance of an express power, which necessarily and in its direct operation impairs the obligation of contracts, is inconsistent with the spirit of the Constitution."[344]

Accordingly, my opinion for the majority of the Court found that Griswold was not required to accept Greenbacks from Hepburn in payment of their note, made before the passage of the Legal Tender Acts.

- $ $ $ -

- $ -

Once I completed my reading and sat down, Sam Miller rose to offer his dissent in open Court.

With respect to the Constitution's prohibition on the power of states to "coin money, emit bills of credit, or make anything but gold and silver coin a tender in payment of debts," Miller emphasized that "[n]o such prohibition is placed upon the power of Congress on this subject, though there are ... matters expressly forbidden to Congress; but neither this of legal tender, nor of the power to emit bills of credit, or to impair the obligation of contracts, is among them."[345]

Sam attacked the notion that the Necessary and Proper Clause restricts federal power. Such a doctrine, he stated, means that "when an act of Congress is brought to the test of this clause of the Constitution, its necessity must be absolute and its adaptation to the conceded purpose unquestionable."[346] This Court has steadfastly denied this position, he said.[347] Quoting Chief Justice Marshall in *McCullough v. Maryland*, Sam wrote:

[The Necessary and Proper Clause] provision is made in a Constitution intended to endure for ages to come, and consequently to be adapted to various crises of human affairs. To have prescribed the means by which the government should in all future time execute its powers would have been to change entirely the character of the instrument and give it the properties of a legal code. It would have been an unwise attempt to provide by immutable rules for exigencies which, if foreseen at all, must have been but dimly, and which can best be provided for as they occur. To have declared that the best means shall not be used, but those alone without which the power given would be nugatory, would have been to deprive the legislature of the capacity to avail itself of experience, to exercise its reason, and to accommodate its legislation to circumstances.[348]

Sam recounted the benefits that the Federal Government received during the late war when the Legal Tender Acts were enacted:

It furnished instantly a means of paying the soldiers in the field, and filled the coffers of the commissary and quartermaster. It furnished a medium for the payment of private debts, as well as public, at a time when gold was being rapidly withdrawn from circulation and the state bank currency was becoming worthless. It furnished the means to the capitalist of buying the bonds of the government. It stimulated trade, revived the drooping energies of the country, and restored confidence to the public mind.[349]

Sam answered the key rationale to my majority opinion thus:

It is now said, however, in the calm retrospect of these events, that Treasury notes suitable for circulation as money, bearing on their face the pledge of the United States for their ultimate payment in coin, would, if not equally efficient, have answered the requirement of the occasion without being made a lawful tender for debts.

But what was needed was something more than the credit of the government. That had been stretched to its utmost tension, and was clearly no longer sufficient in the simple form of borrowing money. Is there any reason to believe that the mere change in the form of the security given would have revived this sinking credit? On the contrary, all experience shows that a currency not redeemable promptly in coin, but dependent on the credit of a promisor whose resources are rapidly diminishing while his liabilities are increasing, soon sinks to the dead level of worthless paper. As no man would have been compelled to take it in payment of debts, as it bore no interest, as its period of redemption would have been remote and uncertain, this must have been the inevitable fate of any extensive issue of such notes.

But when by law they were made to discharge the function of paying debts, they had a perpetual credit or value equal to the amount of all the debts, public and private, in the country. If they were never redeemed, as they never have been, they still paid debts at their par value, and for this purpose were then, and always have been, eagerly sought by the people. To say, then, that this quality of legal tender was not necessary to their usefulness seems to be unsupported by any sound view of the situation.[350]

- $ $ $ -

- $ -

Justice Grier resigned from the Court on February 1, before our reading in open Court. Although he was not present on the day of the reading as he was bedridden and near death, I relayed to the audience before us that he "stated his judgment to be that the legal tender clause, properly construed, has no application to debts contracted prior to its enactment, but that upon the construction given to the act by the other judges he concurred in the opinion that the clause, so far as it makes United States notes a legal tender for such debts, is not warranted by the Constitution."[351] Less than a year later, he died.

Chapter Twenty-eight – Hard Money Gets Reversed

THROUGHOUT THE CIVIL WAR AND ITS aftermath, the Supreme Court suffered much upheaval. The Taney Court of 1861 comprised eight Justices, four of whom were Northerners and four of whom were Southerners. It was the disastrous Court of *Dred Scott v. Sanford* that precipitated the war itself.

By 1862, the Taney Court had been pared down by two deaths, one a Northerner and the other a Southerner, to six Justices. It was still split evenly between the North and the South. Taney continued to hold sway, striking down as many of Lincoln's war initiatives as he could convince his colleagues to join. In that year, Lincoln appointed three Northerners as new Justices to break Taney's Southern stranglehold and revive the nine-Justice Court.

The following year, on May 20, 1863, Lincoln solidified the Northern majority on the Court by appointing Stephen Field to be a tenth Justice. Two months later, on July 23, a Congress that was now satisfied with the Court's seven-to-three pro-Unionist makeup amended the Judiciary Act to freeze all future appointments to the Court unless, by death or resignation, its number fell to six Justices. Chief Justice Taney died in 1864 and was replaced by me. We were now an eight-to-two pro-Unionist Court of ten Justices.

Justice Catron died in 1865 and Justice Wayne died in 1867. In accordance with the revised Judiciary Act, these two last Southerners were not replaced, leaving us with eight Justices, all pro-Union.

After the war, our chief judicial concern turned from slavery to money. Hard-money Justices dominated the soft-money ones by five-to-three by the time that the *Hepburn* case was heard.

Our ruling in *Hepburn* aroused a furor in Congress and the White House. I was pilloried in the press for my inconsistent position in *Hepburn* compared to my actions as Secretary of the Treasury during the war. President Grant and his entire cabinet were against it. They were greatly concerned that the decision would reduce the nation's money supply and ruin the economy, particularly if the country needed to print money during an emergency,

It wasn't long before the soft-money men finagled a fix. The Judiciary Act was revised again on April 10, 1869, to set the number of Justices at nine. When Justice Grier, a hard-money man, resigned in February 1870, after the *Hepburn* decision was issued, President Grant picked two soft-money men, Justices Strong and Bradley, to fill the two vacant seats. They were railroad lawyers – railroads, always in debt to banks when constructing new tracks, favored depreciation that would lower their cost of debt.[352] Soft-money men now dominated hard-money men on the Court by five-to-four.

The soft-money forces in Washington set to work on reversing *Hepburn*. Feeling compelled to justify my actions at Treasury, I said in my opinion for the Court in *Hepburn*:

> *It is not surprising that amid the tumult of the late civil war, and under the influence of apprehensions for the safety of the Republic almost universal, different views, never before entertained by American statesmen or jurists, were adopted by many. The time was not favorable to considerate reflection upon the constitutional limits of legislative or executive authority. If power was assumed from patriotic motives, the*

assumption found ready justification in patriotic hearts. Many who doubted yielded their doubts; many who did not doubt were silent. Some who were strongly averse to making government notes a legal tender felt themselves constrained to acquiesce in the views of the advocates of the measure. Not a few who then insisted upon its necessity, or acquiesced in that view, have, since the return of peace and under the influence of the calmer time, reconsidered their conclusions, and now concur in those which we have just announced. These conclusions seem to us to be fully sanctioned by the letter and spirit of the Constitution.[353]

Justice Strong took his seat after Grier's death, in March 1870. Justice Bradley was sworn in on March 23 and took his seat on the Court the next day. One day later, U.S. Attorney General Ebenezer R. Hoar made a motion to the Court to set two Court of Claims cases, *Latham v. U.S.* and *Deming v. U.S.*, for simultaneous oral argument, and to reconsider the legal tender issue.

The *Latham* and *Deming* cases had been passed over in previous Supreme Court terms, and we were prepared to do the same during the December 1869 Term. The lawyers in the cases, including counsel for the government, had long-since agreed that if there was any legal tender issue in them, the rule then being considered in the *Hepburn* case would apply when it was announced. Nevertheless, after *Hepburn* issued, Hoar was sorely pressured to make his motion despite the agreement not to re-litigate the legal tender issue.[354]

Saturday, March 26, 1870, was our normal judicial conference day. Attorney General Hoar's motion was on my agenda.

"Gentlemen," I said at the conference, "I believe that we should reject this motion. The legal tender issue should not be re-argued in these cases. *Hepburn* should stand."

"I concur," said Justices Nelson, Clifford, and Field almost simultaneously, who had joined with me on *Hepburn*.

"I cannot agree, Chief," said Sam Miller, the principal *Hepburn* dissenter. "The Attorney General is clearly expressing a matter of important public interest. It would be unjust to reject his motion."

"Agreed," his *Hepburn* co-dissenters Swayne and Davis chimed in.

Strong and Bradley looked at one another and remained silent. Having not participated in *Hepburn*, they opted to let the Justices who had done so duke it out.

"It is highly irregular to reconsider an issue in the very next case during the same term in which it was decided," I objected. To me, politics were interfering in a matter of jurisprudence. "The lawyers in these cases have already stipulated that *Hepburn* would apply to these cases. The Attorney General cannot simply override agreed-upon precedent in this way!"

"These Court of Claims cases are not the same as *Hepburn*, Chief," Sam Miller replied. "We have been dealing with the legal tender issue piecemeal up to now, and the Attorney General is simply asking us to continue to do so. We decided in cases before *Hepburn* that state taxes may be payable only in specie notwithstanding the Legal Tender Acts, and that contracts that stipulate payment in specie must be honored despite those Acts.

"*Hepburn* decided only that debts made before the Acts were passed must be paid in specie," Sam continued. "Now we must consider whether Federal contract claims must be paid in specie. There is no overarching rule in *Hepburn* that requires us to avoid the legal tender issue now. And we are not bound by a lawyers' stipulation if we disagree with it."

We haggled over this matter at great length. Ultimately, a motion was made to fix a date for hearing the cases, including the legal tender issue, and it passed, unsurprisingly, by a vote of five-to-four –the three *Hepburn* dissenters plus Bradley and Strong on one side, the remaining *Hepburn* majority (including myself) on the other.[355]

But on the date of the hearing, we learned that the attorneys for the private parties had decided in the interim to seek dismissal of both cases. A surprised Attorney General Hoar objected strenuously to the dismissal and demanded to argue the case, but since the private parties had made the claims against the government, their dismissal would relieve the government of all liability. We justices disagreed with one another on what to do, of course, and I called for us to withdraw for consultation.

Once in chambers, Sam Miller piped up, "The private lawyers have sandbagged the Attorney General! We must hear these cases!"

"Just one minute, Brother Miller," I said to him testily. I was not going to condone any more of these political shenanigans by the soft-money lobby. "It has been the rule in this Court since 1852," I said, "that no re-argument will be granted in any case unless a member of the Court who concurred in the judgment desires it. Not one of us in the majority in *Hepburn* has intimated any desire for re-argument.[356]

"That is the end of the matter!" I bellowed. "The private parties have every right to have their claims against the government dismissed. Hoar cannot force them to argue a case that they don't want to make! I will not kowtow to naked political pressure on this Court!

"I think we're done here," I barked, glaring at each Justice one by one. They all nodded sheepishly in agreement, including Sam.

When we returned to the courtroom, I announced that it was "the unanimous judgment of the Court that the appellants had a right to have their appeals dismissed, and they are both DISMISSED ACCORDINGLY."[357]

- $ $ $ -

- $ -

That, of course, was not the end of the matter.

In the very next term commencing December 1870, the cases of *Knox v. Lee* and *Parker v. Davis* arrived.[358] The *"Legal Tender Cases,"* as they came to be known, were heard simultaneously.

Knox v. Lee came from western Texas. Mrs. Lee, a loyal citizen of the United States and a resident of Pennsylvania, owned a flock of sheep in Texas. At the outbreak of the civil war, she had left her sheep in the charge of her Texas shepherd. In March 1863, the Confederates confiscated and sold the sheep to Mr. Knox as the property of an "alien enemy." Once the war ended, Mrs. Lee sued Mr. Knox for trespass and conversion of her herd. The value of the herd was called into question, and Mrs. Lee demanded payment in gold and/or silver rather than in Greenbacks. The court below allowed Mr. Knox to pay in Greenbacks, and this appeal to our Court followed.[359]

Parker v. Davis arose in Massachusetts. Davis sued Parker for specific performance of a contract to sell land to Davis upon payment of a given sum of money. The contract was dated and the suit brought before passage of any of the Legal Tender Acts. The Supreme Court of Massachusetts ordered Davis to pay into the court the required sum, upon which Parker would execute a deed to him of the land in question. Davis paid the sum in Greenbacks, which Parker refused to accept. Parker, therefore, did not execute a deed. The court ordered Parker to do so, thereby recognizing the Greenbacks, and Parker appealed to this Court from that decree.

To my dismay, our Court upheld the Legal Tender Acts by our new soft-money majority of five-to-four. Justice Strong wrote the majority opinion with a concurrence by Justice Bradley. I wrote a dissent in which Justices Nelson, Clifford, and Field joined.

Figure 65: Associate Justice William Strong (PD)

The issue that the Court addressed was the same one as in *Hepburn v. Griswold*: Were the Legal Tender Acts constitutional when applied to contracts made before their passage; and are they valid as applicable to debts contracted since their enactment? Strong emphasized that *Hepburn* would produce disastrous results, causing "throughout the country, great business derangement, widespread distress, and the rankest injustice." U.S. Treasury Notes "have become the universal measure of values," he said. With *Hepburn*, "the government has become an instrument of the grossest injustice; all debtors are loaded with an obligation it was never contemplated they should assume; a large percentage is added to every debt, and such must become the demand for gold to satisfy contracts, that ruinous sacrifices, general distress, and bankruptcy may be expected."[360]

The new majority did not see in the Constitution's gaps any limitation on the Federal Government's powers, as we in the *Hepburn* majority saw it. "We do not expect to find in a constitution minute details," Strong wrote. "It is necessarily brief and comprehensive. It prescribes outlines, leaving the filling up to be deduced from the outlines."

As for the non-enumerated powers derived from the Necessary and Proper Clause, they were useful tools for the future that were "intended to confer upon the government the power of self-preservation," Strong wrote. He quoted Chief Justice John Marshall in *Cohens v. Bank of Virginia*:

> *A constitution is framed for ages to come, and is designed to approach immortality as near as mortality can approach it. Its course cannot always be tranquil. It is exposed to storms and tempests, and its framers must be unwise statesmen indeed, if they have not provided it, as far as its nature will permit, with the means of self-preservation from the perils it is sure to encounter.*[361]

"[I]t is not indispensable to the existence of any power claimed for the Federal Government," Strong argued, "that it can be found specified in the words of the Constitution, or clearly and directly traceable to some one of the specified powers."[362]

Civil war created the exigency that made it necessary for Congress to assert powers that might not necessarily be asserted in peacetime, Strong wrote. "It is not to be denied that acts may be adapted to the exercise of lawful power, and appropriate to it, in seasons of exigency, which would be inappropriate at other times," he said.[363] It did not matter that Treasury demand-notes without the legal tender clause would have accomplished the same goal as notes with that legend, as I had said in *Hepburn*:

> *But admitting it to be true, what does it prove? Nothing more than that Congress had the choice of means for a legitimate end, each appropriate, and adapted to that end, though, perhaps, in different degrees. What then? Can this court say that it ought to have adopted one rather than the other? Is it our province to decide that the means selected were beyond the constitutional power of Congress, because we may think that other means to the same ends would have been more appropriate and equally efficient? That would be to assume legislative power, and to disregard the accepted rules for construing the Constitution.*[364]

The lack of an express power given to the Federal Government, such as the power to print paper money rather than gold and silver coin, did not imply to the majority "that because certain powers over the currency are expressly given to Congress, all other powers relating to the same subject are impliedly forbidden."[365] Quite to the contrary, Strong argued, "there are some considerations touching these clauses which tend to show that if any implications are to be deduced from them, they are of an enlarging rather than a restraining character."[366]

This was the first time, in my experience, that a majority of the Supreme Court of the United States had ever read the Constitution to confer on the Federal Government *enlarged* powers rather than *restrained* powers. Indeed, Strong went so far as to hold that "when one of such powers was expressly denied to the States only, it was for the purpose of rendering the Federal power *more complete and exclusive.*"[367] This statement, to me, was quite a leap.

The majority went on to hold that the Legal Tender Acts are not unconstitutional because they impair the obligation of contracts, as we found in *Hepburn*. "[T]he obligation of a contract to pay money is to pay that which the law shall recognize as money when the payment is to be made," Strong wrote.[368] Nor were they takings of property without just compensation. Pointing to an 1834 act that reduced the amount of gold in $1,000 "Eagle" coins by six per cent, Strong remarked that

> *The creditor who had a thousand dollars due him on the 31st day of July, 1834 (the day before the act took effect), was entitled to a thousand dollars of coined gold of the weight and fineness of the then existing coinage. The day after, he was entitled only to a sum six per cent. less in weight and in market value, or to a smaller number of silver dollars. Yet he would have been a bold man who had asserted that, because of this, the obligation of the contract was impaired, or that private property was taken without compensation or without due process of law.*[369]

Strong wrapped up by pointing out that the value of a coin is a concept, not something intrinsic to it:

> *[V]alue is an ideal thing. The coinage acts fix [a one-dollar coin's] unit as a dollar; but the gold or silver thing we call a dollar is, in no sense, a standard of a dollar. It is a representative of it. There might never have been a piece of money of the denomination of a dollar. There never was a pound sterling coined until 1815, if we except a few coins struck in the reign of Henry VIII, almost immediately debased, yet it has been the unit of British currency for many generations. It is, then, a mistake to regard the legal tender acts as either fixing a standard of value or regulating money values, or making that money which has no intrinsic value.*
> [370]

Thus, the majority found that the Legal Tender Acts were constitutional as applied to contracts made either before or after their passage. The majority declared *Hepburn v. Griswold* to be overruled. By way of explanation for overruling a prior precedent so quickly, Strong noted that *Hepburn* "was decided by a divided court, and by a court having a less number of judges than the law then in existence provided this court shall have. These cases have been heard before a full court, and they have received our most careful consideration."[371] This statement surprised and angered me. We had been an eight-Justice court or even less for quite some time; were all of our decisions that had been rendered during that period wrongly decided as a consequence?

- $ $ $ -

- $ -

In the hope that some future Supreme Court might see the light and reverse this bad decision of a bare and politically-motivated majority, I wrote a dissent to justify as best as I possibly could the reasoning of the *Hepburn* decision. Justices Clifford and Field also wrote dissents.

As we had all agreed to before, I urged that "Congress may not adopt any means for the execution of an express power that Congress may see fit to adopt." I pointed out that the means "must be a necessary and proper means within the fair meaning of the rule" as Justice Marshall had expressed it in *McCullough v. Maryland*. To me, a paper dollar was only a *promise* to pay a "real" dollar. I said in dissent, therefore, that "an act of Congress making promises to pay dollars legal tender as coined dollars in payment of pre-existing debts" did not meet Justice Marshall's test. [372]

I read this rule to mean that the wording of the Necessary and Proper Clause was "intended to have 'a sense at once admonitory and directory,'" and that the Tenth Amendment to the Constitution "'was intended to have a like admonitory and directory sense'" to reserve to the States or the people all powers not delegated to the United States by the Constitution, nor prohibited by it to the States. In other words, these clauses of the Constitution were meant to *limit* the powers of the Federal Government, not to *expand* them, and to leave all other powers to the States respectively, or to the People. [373]

To me, there was "no connection between the express power to coin money and the inference that the government may, in any contingency, make its securities perform the functions of coined money, as a legal tender in payment of debts." [374]

I endeavored to explain my actions as Secretary of the Treasury that led to the issuance and circulation of Greenbacks. In no report that I made to Congress, I pointed out, "was the expedient of making the notes of the United States a legal tender suggested."[375] I recommended to Congress at that time "no mere paper money scheme, but on the contrary a series of measures looking to a safe and gradual return to gold and silver as the only permanent basis, standard, and measure of the value recognized by the Constitution." [376]

Nonetheless, before I made that report to Congress, the Legal Tender Act became law. I was against it, but at the same time I "was very solicitous for the passage of the bill to authorize the issue of United States notes then pending," and "under these circumstances" I expressed the opinion to Committee of Ways and Means "that it was necessary." It was necessary, I explained, "to the payment of the army and the navy and to all the purposes for which the government uses money." I admitted in my present dissent, however, "that this opinion was erroneous," and that I did not hesitate to declare it at this later time.[377]

Having said that, I turned to whether the issuance of Greenbacks was "necessary and proper" and hence constitutional. It was not so as a means to the execution of the power to borrow money. Notes redeemable in coin at a later date would have circulated just as well without being recognized as legal tender. Any premium that the notes required to equalize their value with specie would be provided in the prices of goods. [378] As long as the government ultimately made good on its promise to redeem them in coin, they would hold their value, and such notes in circulation at the time did so.

I criticized the notion that declaring Greenbacks to be legal tender enhances their value:

> *When the government compels the people to receive its notes,*
> *it virtually declares that it does not expect them to be*

*received without compulsion. It practically represents itself
insolvent. This certainly does not improve the value of its
notes. It is an element of depreciation. In addition, it creates
a powerful interest in the debtor class and in the purchasers
of bonds to depress to the lowest point the credit of the notes.
The cheaper these become, the easier the payment of debts,
and the more profitable the investments in bonds bearing
coin interest. ... But the apparent benefit is a delusion and
the necessity imaginary. In their legitimate use, the notes
are hurt not helped by being made a legal tender. The legal
tender quality is only valuable for the purposes of dishonesty.
Every honest purpose is answered as well and better without
it.*[379]

Thus, I argued, making such notes legal tender did nothing to
enhance its value and was not at all "necessary and proper" means to
exercise an express power of the government. Indeed, I implied, such
notes are *immoral*.

I concluded my dissent with arguments that the Legal Tender Acts
constituted a taking of private property for public use without just
compensation, in violation of the Fifth Amendment to the
Constitution. I also maintained that the Legal Tender Acts
interfered with the obligations of contracts.

- $ $ $ -

- $ -

After the majority opinion and the concurrences and dissents were
read in open Court, Justice Strong approached me as we were
hanging up our robes in the Cloak Room.

"Chief," he said to me, "I listened carefully to your explanation of the economics of legal tender notes as you see it. Where did you derive that rationale?"

"Why, it is such a commonplace, Bill," I replied, "In any transaction, there is an exchange of value. It is a fundamental concept of contract law. Where is the 'detriment to the promisee' and 'benefit to the promisor' if the promisee hands over only paper as consideration for the promisor's labor or product? It is trading something for nothing!"

"How did you find that economic theory to match up with your experience with Greenbacks when you were Secretary of the Treasury?" Strong asked me.

I thought for a bit. "Well, Bill, that's hard to say. The gold premium over the face-value of coin, which we tracked carefully, fluctuated but generally increased over the course of the war. After it was over, the premium dropped back to par, more or less."

"And of course," Strong said, "the U.S. Notes experienced the same rate of inflation because their face-value was the same as gold coin, am I right?"

"Yes, that's right," I replied. "A dollar was a dollar, no matter what form it was in, so being in coin or paper didn't matter much to the value of a dollar."

"Would you say, Chief," Strong continued, "that the gold premium fluctuated as a result of events, such as military victories and defeats, and even your resignation as Treasury Secretary; or did it do so by reason of the composition of the money itself; that is, in coin or in paper?"

"It was definitely caused by events," I admitted. I was beginning to see where Bill was going with this.

"Now, U.S. Demand Notes circulated as currency, but they were promises to pay in gold or silver at a later date, right?"

"Yes, Bill."

"So, if events started to look like the U.S. would be defeated, people would worry about the future likelihood that the Demand Notes would be redeemed, and the gold premium over them would rise, wouldn't you say?"

"That's true, Bill."

"But a Greenback doesn't work that way, Chief," Bill replied. "A one-dollar Greenback note is a dollar no matter what the gold premium is. Its par value is always the same. But a Demand Note's par value varies *according to the government's ability to keep its promise to redeem it.* You said so yourself in your dissent. There is no such promise for the Government to keep concerning a Greenback. Am I right?"

I was silent.

"Y'see, Chief," Bill Strong continued, "paper money that is legal tender by law is as good to a willing buyer and a willing seller of a good or service as a gold coin is. It is worth the amount that is stamped on it. Gold coins are shaved when the price of gold rises because the gold in the coin is worth more than the coin's face-value. That's got to do with the worth of the metal, not the worth of a dollar. Prices fluctuate because the relative value of goods and services changes, not because of the relative value of goods and services to the dollar.

"What I'm saying, Chief, is that we don't need gold and silver coins at all in order to carry on our economy," Sam said. "A paper dollar will do just fine. If everybody recognizes that a legal paper dollar is equal to a dollar in worth, then it can be used to buy goods and services and its composition in gold or silver or paper don't matter!

"And one thing more, Chief," Bill said. "No country can fight a war without issuing *fiat* money. England had irredeemable paper money for fifty years while it fought Napoleon. Look where England is today. You can't deny America the ability to preserve itself against its enemies just because you can't find the exact words in the Constitution for it!"

Bill turned without further word and walked away from me to join his colleagues in the Justices' Smoke Room, where they always congregated for Cuban cigars and Kentucky bourbons after a Supreme Court hearing.

- $ $ $ -

- $ -

After dinner at home, I sat in my easy chair before the fire, alone, late into the night. I thought deeply about what Bill said.

I thought back to what Peter Cooper had said to me many years ago. It was the exact same thing. And Bill Harrington felt the same way. Once the war began, our economy expanded exponentially. There was way more that we had to do than we did before the war had begun. The only way that we were able to accomplish that task was to expand the money supply to meet the expanded economy's need for money. People were working hard, creating great value. Soldiers were fighting in the field; sailors were fighting on ships. More goods and services were produced in the United States at that time than at any time before.

There was not enough gold and silver in the world to mint the number of coins that we needed to pay the enormous debts we were incurring. Something had to replace gold and silver, and that was paper and the law.

A piece of specially-produced paper with a fancy design (and my portrait) on it, labeled with a dollar denomination and the legend that "This Note is legal tender for all debts, public and private," passes from hand to hand in return for goods and services that are worth the dollar amount that is exchanged. The composition of the coin or paper that is passed is of minimal importance if the Greenback is considered worth the good or service it buys, and can be exchanged thereafter for goods and services of like value. That is the definition of "currency."

Gold and silver are not storehouses of value that must be used to make the economy run. They are merely metals that carry a price per ounce, and that price varies according to what the market will pay for them. Indeed, they are far more expensive to use to create money than paper is, and the savings from the cheaper production of paper money is a benefit to the Government that known in banking finance as "seigniorage."

These thoughts occupied my mind that night, but they were not what was keeping me awake. What robbed me of sleep was that I was growing very sick.

PART SIX
LESSONS

Chapter Twenty-nine – The Legacy of Salmon P. Chase

B Y THE TIME OF THE HEARING OF THE HEPBURN CASE, Sam Chase was an unwell man. He was suffering from heart disease, high blood pressure, malaria, and diabetes.[380] The year before, he had suffered a mild heart attack. Later, he suffered a stroke on a train in New York. His right side was paralyzed from that stroke and he could hardly speak. He convalesced for a couple of months at William Sprague's home, Canonchet, on the Narragansett Bay in Rhode Island. [381]

Chase's condition rose and fell. On good days, he would have a fine appetite that he would satiate with a filling meal, but later in the day might suffer a mild heart attack.[382] He felt well enough to return to his duties in Washington and participated in the decisions of several important cases. He would see his younger daughter, Nettie, marry William Hoyt, a wealthy banker and cousin of William Sprague's. But he would witness Sprague's marriage to his older daughter, Kate, fall apart.[383]

In May 1873, after the Court term ended, Chase traveled to New York to stay at the Hoyts' house in Manhattan. On the morning of May 6, his valet entered Chase's bedroom and found that he had suffered another, massive stroke. He died at 10 a.m. the next day, May 7, surrounded by his family and physicians.[384]

- $ $ $ -

- $ -

United States Notes, the famous "Greenbacks," continued to be issued by the Treasury until January 1971. They are still legal tender today, although not many are found in circulation.

Figure 66: $10,000 U.S. Gold Certificate, Series 1934—Front and Back (PD)

"Gold Certificates" were issued by the Treasury commencing in 1865, and were redeemable by the Treasury in gold coins. They were a popular means of paying interest on debts and tariff duties because they were more convenient to do so than gold coin, which was required by law for those debts. The portrait of Salmon P. Chase was featured on the $10,000 Gold Certificate.

In 1933, when the private ownership of gold was outlawed in the United States by an Executive Order issued by President Franklin Roosevelt, Gold Certificates went out of circulation. Private ownership of gold was not reinstated until December 31, 1974.

During and after the civil war, Greenbacks were not accepted in California and Oregon, where gold was plentiful. But they acted readily as currency in the rest of the Union, where gold was in very short supply. As we have seen, the premium of gold to Greenbacks was high and rose or fell with the successes and failures of the Union Army. They could pay for contracts denominated in dollars, and as the Legal Tender Cases held, they had to be accepted for such purposes at their face-value.

Greenbacks held their value relatively well compared to Confederate dollar certificates, which the Confederates promised to redeem into gold after the war ended. Confederate dollars, too, rose and fell in value with Confederate victories and defeats. By war's end, they were worthless.

Greenbacks, circulating at the same time as Gold Certificates, initially could be exchanged for the latter, or for gold coin, only at a discount from their face-value. After Congress passed the "Specie Resumption Act" that became effective in 1879, however, the Treasury began redeeming Greenbacks at face-value in gold and silver, which equalized their value with gold and silver coins of the same denominations..

Greenbacks remained a hot topic long after the Civil War. The "Greenback Party," which nominated Horace Greeley for President in 1876, ran on the platform of removing the U.S. from the gold standard and making the Greenback the fiat currency of America. Greeley's party lost in that controversial election, but the currency question remained as banks fought to maintain the gold standard while farmers, laborers, and other debtors fought for paper money. William Jennings Bryan, the famous "Boy Orator of the River Platte," ran for the Democrats in the 1896 Presidential election, having won the nomination after *making his famous "Cross of Gold" speech at that party's nominating convention. This was its ringing ending:*

> If they dare to come out in the open field and defend the gold standard as a good thing, we will fight them to the uttermost. Having behind us the producing masses of this nation and the world, supported by the commercial interests, the laboring interests, and the toilers everywhere, we will answer their demand for a gold standard by saying to them: You shall not press down upon the brow of labor this crown of thorns, you shall not crucify mankind upon a cross of gold.[385]

Figure 67: William Jennings Bryan, after "Cross of Gold" Speech, hoisted on shoulders of delegates at Chicago Democratic Convention, 1896 (PD)

The Treasury's redemption of Gold Certificates and U.S. Notes with gold coin did not end until 1933, when President Roosevelt ended the practice and required all gold held in private hands to be turned into the Treasury as a way to combat the hoarding of gold during the Depression. Thereafter, Gold Certificates were exchanged only by intra-governmental transactions. Eventually, the paper Gold

Certificates were phased out and replaced by wire transfers between electronic accounts of the Treasury and the Federal Reserve.

In response to raging inflationary pressures that were depleting the Treasury's gold supply, President Nixon took the country off the gold standard in January 1971. As a result, the primary currency circulating in the United States today is the "Federal Reserve Note," which is backed by bank reserves that the national banks deposit in the Federal Reserve. These accounts are held electronically. This action has allowed our economy to expand to meet the needs of our large population, a capability that all the limited availability of gold and silver in the world cannot match.

If the practice of exchanging currency sounds bafflingly like circular reasoning to you, that's because it is. A One-Dollar Federal Reserve Note is what it is solely because the law prescribes that it can buy one dollar's worth of goods and services in the United States; nothing more. If you want to "redeem" it, a bank will give you four quarters, or ten dimes, or 100 pennies; you won't get any gold. Of course, nobody goes to banks to do that, because the Federal Reserve Note will buy an apple or two just as well, perhaps even more readily, than gold nuggets. Federal Reserve Notes are "money," and after all, what is money for?

As the Hepburn v. Griswold *and* Legal Tender *cases show, the power of the Federal Government to issue paper money was a hotly-contested legal issue after the Civil War. The Constitution expressly empowers the government only to "coin" money, and the jurists of that day interpreted that express power to exclude, by negative inference, the issuance of paper money. The* Legal Tender *cases did not change the constitutional definition of the words "coin money," but instead applied the Constitution's "Necessary and Proper" Clause to imply from its relevant express powers that the government had the power to print and circulate paper money as legal tender for all debts, public and private.*

That legal gyration possibly would not be necessary today, in the world of computer and electronic-transfer technology. "Coin" would probably be interpreted by modern judges to imply, by definition, to "print on paper" or "transfer electronically," and would therefore be treated as an "express" power of the government. That is because, as Chief Justice John Marshall recognized in the earlier case of Cohens v. Bank of Virginia:

> A constitution is framed for ages to come, and is designed to approach immortality as near as mortality can approach it. Its course cannot always be tranquil. It is exposed to storms and tempests, and its framers must be unwise statesmen indeed, if they have not provided it, as far as its nature will permit, with the means of self-preservation from the perils it is sure to encounter. [386]

These words of Chief Justice John Marshall suggest that there are limits to the notion of "originalism" as the right way to interpret the language of the Constitution. The modern judicial fixation on so-called "history and tradition" for the purpose of understanding 18th-century constitutional language cannot be applied so narrowly as to ignore the realities of modern life. Today's courts go too far when they apply the language of colonial America to semi-automatic weapons in the same way as one-shot muskets, or to massive Ponzi schemes in computerized financial markets as akin to common-law fraud in feudal England.

Recently, the Supreme Court has started to realize and accept this limitation. It applied it to the controversial, oft-litigated "right to keep and bear arms" of the Second Amendment. In United States v. Rahimi, *the Court held that this right does not bar courts from issuing restraining orders against owning guns in certain modern-day circumstances of violence and danger. To quote Chief Justice John Roberts, who wrote the opinion for an 8-1 majority of the Court:*

[S]ome courts have misunderstood the methodology of our recent Second Amendment cases. These precedents were not meant to suggest a law trapped in amber. As we explained in [*District of Columbia v. Heller*, 554 U.S. 570, 582 (2008)], for example, the reach of the Second Amendment is not limited only to those arms that were in existence at the founding. Rather, it "extends, prima facie, to all instruments that constitute bearable arms, even those that were not [yet] in existence." By that same logic, the Second Amendment permits more than just those regulations identical to ones that could be found in 1791. Holding otherwise would be as mistaken as applying the protections of the right only to muskets and sabers.[387]

It is refreshing to know that at least some Supreme Court Justices today are wise enough to credit Chief Justice John Marshall's rationale of 200 years ago.

Hence, the reliance of our massive modern economy on Federally-backed "fiat" paper and electronic currency is now a well-established and stable constitutional principle.

- $ $ $ -

- $ -

There is today an economic concept known as "Modern Monetary Theory." It says that countries like the United States that use "fiat money" – that is, paper or electronic domestically-circulated currency that is not backed by gold or silver, but instead is prescribed by law as legal tender for all debts, public and private – can never run out of money because they can always create more by statute. As long as the government takes effective steps to control inflation, fiat *money should* maintain its value for the purposes it serves in the economy.[388] *Not every country can do this; only countries with "sovereignty" over their currencies, such as Japan, the United Kingdom, Australia, Canada, and some others, can do so.[389] Countries that spend and borrow in their own currencies, not in the currencies of other countries, are capable of this feat.[390]*

This is precisely what Salmon P. Chase accomplished as Secretary of the Treasury, 160 years before "MMT" (the acronym for Modern Monetary Theory) became a much-discussed economic topic. Greenbacks were used to pay soldiers, sailors, and military vendors and could be used by them as legal tender to pay their debts. They worked as currency because the law required their acceptance. Greenbacks could not pay foreign debts; those had to be paid in currency that the foreign party would accept, usually gold or silver. By the same token, U.S. tariffs had to be paid in gold or silver because the Federal Government expected foreign importers to pay its tariffs in the same manner as their own countries expected their own tariffs to be paid.

It has been suggested that America's fiat *currency, if issued in sufficient quantities, could wipe out our national deficits and even our national debt by simply paying them off with such Notes. We could just flood creditors with paper dollars and eliminate our liabilities.*

This trick of using currency's characteristic of being "legal tender for all debts, public and private" to eliminate national debt has a logical ring to it, but it is a false one. The need of the government to control inflation of fiat *currency throws a wrench into the logic. There is no way to issue such large amounts of* fiat *notes to pay off the trillions of dollars of deficit and debt without setting off an "atom bomb" of runaway inflation, not seen since Weimar Germany tried it to its detriment after World War I. The money supply of a country must be carefully managed to maintain its usefulness to the economy.*

The notion is often bandied about in the U.S. Capitol that Social Security, Medicare, and other discretionary and military programs should be cut back to save money and reduce the deficit. These demands fail to account for the realities of having a fiat *national currency.*

The national debt may always increase in the future because, unlike households, the Federal Government exists in perpetuity and can always pay its debts. It can pay off old debt and interest by issuing new debt – essentially, by foisting the debts of past generations on the wallets of future generations. But even that calamity never will happen – generations that forever foist old debts off to future generations never pay those debts, and their progeny will do the same.

This unending validity of the U.S. debt, our Constitution says in the Fourteenth Amendment, "shall not be questioned."[391] *So our Constitution promises us that the Federal Government will* never *default on its debt.* Period.

If money must be had to pay Social Security benefits and Medicare costs, fiat *money may be issued to do so as long as the government monitors inflation. Weimar Germany, in the throes of a depression after World War I, could not contain the inflationary balloon that soared out of control. America, fortunately, has not suffered the fate of Germany in warfare – and one must have hope that it never will.*

There has occasionally been talk of the U.S. Government minting a "trillion-dollar platinum coin" and transferring it to the Treasury for the purpose of creating an accounting "asset" that eliminates the Treasury's need to obtain Congressional approval to issue new debt – which periodically triggers the political bugaboo of "raising the debt ceiling."

The Federal law governing the minting of coin, 31 U.S.C. 5112(k), provides that "[t]he Secretary [of the Treasury] may mint and issue *platinum bullion coins and proof platinum coins in accordance with such specifications, designs, varieties, quantities, denominations, and inscriptions as the Secretary, in the Secretary's discretion, may prescribe from time to time." So, the argument goes, the Secretary can mint and issue a platinum coin with a face-value of $1,000,000,000,000, transfer the value of the coin over its production cost (i.e., its "seigniorage") to the Federal Reserve, and allow the Federal Reserve to retire old debt to well below the debt ceiling, allowing plenty of room to issue new debt.[392]*

It is a neat trick which threads the needles of government finance that prick so much political blood-letting. The idea has been attacked and mocked, but has not been totally debunked as of this writing. It may very well form the basis for solving the next "debt ceiling controversy" that roils Congress. If nothing else, however, it illustrates the conundrum that the Supreme Court faced in the Legal Tender Cases *(as described fictionally in this book) of "what money is." It is a concept that is more ethereal than relativity, quantum mechanics or the existence of God, but it does not possess the power to end life.*

Afterword

THERE IS MUCH FICTION IN HISTORY. Not even an eye-witness account of a great historical event is wholly accurate. Events are seen and recorded by a single person, through one pair of eyes and ears, wherein biases and prejudices are incorporated and the frame of reference is set.

That is why I write "historical fiction" instead of "history." I do not take it upon myself to present exact facts to you, my dear reader. I seek instead to entertain you with a story that is woven into a grid of facts and embellished where there are gaps in the grid.

I am a retired lawyer, and over the course of my career I have witnessed a significant change in the way that law is expressed by American courts. At one time, courts strove to recite the facts as exactly as they could and then resolve the issues presented by means of logic and reason. They attempted to create remedies that were fit for the modern day.

That genre has passed. Today, judges find answers in the so-called "history and tradition" of the law. They attempt to resolve legal questions now by delving into ancient history to discern the "original" meaning of the words of law that they are interpreting. The objective is to find out how people in medieval times treated the *exact same thing* that the judge is facing in the present day, and to resolve it the *exact same way*.

I find this method to be deficient. History is a pattern of facts with gaps into which *all* writers weave fictions that are meant to entertain the reader. If history is treated as if it were law, one may find oneself basing an execution for murder on a fairy tale.

When I was researching my first book, *The Tenth Seat: A Novel*, I came across an 1854 appellate case from the Supreme Court of California entitled *People v. Hall*, 4 Cal. 399, 1854 WL 765 (Cal. 1854). In it, the defendant/appellant, a "free white citizen of this State, was convicted upon the testimony of Chinese witnesses." The admissibility of the testimony was called into question because of the 1850 statute that governed the criminal proceeding, which said that "No Black, or Mulatto person, or Indian, shall be allowed to give evidence in favor of, or against a white man." It said nothing about the admissibility of the testimony of a Chinese person.

Nonetheless, Chief Judge Murray, writing for the Court, found the statute to be applicable to Chinese witnesses as well. The question turned, he wrote, on "whether the Legislature adopted [these words of the statute] as generic terms, or intended to limit their application to specific types of the human species."

Judge Murray concocted an "ethnology" of the "Asiatic race" that, to him, showed that Indians were in fact racially related to the Chinese, and therefore that "Chinese" were in fact "Indians" within the meaning of the statutory language. He held (with bold font added in some words for emphasis):

> *When Columbus first landed upon the shores of this continent, in his attempt to discover a western passage to the Indies, he imagined that he had accomplished the object of his expedition, and that the Island of San Salvador was one of those Islands of the Chinese sea, lying near the extremity of India, which had been described by navigators.*
>
> *Acting upon this hypothesis, and also perhaps from the similarity of features and physical conformation, **he gave to the Islanders the name of Indians, which appellation***

was universally adopted, and extended to the aboriginals of the New World, as well as of Asia.

From that time, down to a very recent period, the American Indians and the Mongolian, or Asiatic, were regarded as the same type of the human species.

Judge Murray, without citing to any supporting evidence, concluded that the California legislators in 1850 must have known of this then-popular "ethnology" of the Asiatic race, and therefore must have used the word "Indian" in the statute in a so-called "generic" sense, not its specific sense. Why he thought legislators would use a narrow descriptive term so broadly, we are not told. So, he held, Chinese persons were subsumed within the definition of "Indians," and therefore could not legally testify against white men.

Thus do "fractured fairy tales" pass for "history" in this world. I am loath to write a book that purports to be "historical," because I fear that a reader might surmise that something I made up actually took place. To forestall that danger, I profess to write only "historical fiction." Where my statements of fact are based on research, I cite the research in an endnote. Where my statements are imagined, there is no endnote. Read this novel with that admonition in mind.

- $ $ $ -

- $ -

I owe debts of gratitude to several people who aided me in putting this book together. I am grateful to *Wikipedia.org*, the main source of information for me. They have done the world a great service by making information freely available to all in an easily searchable format. They are also amenable to open editing of their entries, which ensures that the most recent and accurate information comes through. There is always someone who will correct a mistaken reference or statement, which was very difficult to expect from the old, rigidly-published encyclopedias of the past.

I am also grateful to *Draft2Digital.com*, an open publishing application that makes it possible for independent authors like myself to reach an extensive book market and attract a wide readership. That has not always been easy, of course, because I am not a well-known celebrity with a juicy story to tell my fans and detractors. I merely seek to convey a story based on history that I hope will interest a reader to learn more about the topic.

I am very thankful to Dr. Stephanie Kelton, a professor of economics and public policy at Stony Brook University, whose book, *The Deficit Myth*, was my inspiration for writing *Greenback*. Dr. Kelton's book describes, in easily-comprehensible fashion, how the *fiat* currency system of the United States works. I was motivated by it to explore how this system came about, its origins in the Civil War financial crisis, and the role of Salmon P. Chase, both at the Treasury Department and the U.S. Supreme Court.

Having myself spent over thirty years as an employee of the Federal Government in a variety of legal capacities, including as an Attorney-Advisor to the U.S. Department of Energy and the U.S. International Trade Commission, and as an Administrative Law Judge for the U.S. Department of Health and Human Services and the Federal Energy Regulatory Commission, I learned first-hand how government works and was eager to convey to readers how it is done every day. The Federal Government is often described darkly in modern political literature as "the Administrative State," a kind of monolith that all must bow down to and from which none can escape its grip. Quite the contrary, it is a workplace full of dedicated people, just like everyone else in America, who like their jobs and seek to satisfy the needs of their public customers. It is personally fulfilling work.

I am particularly grateful to my fellow members of the Maryland Writers Association, particularly its Annapolis Chapter, for offering comradeship and education as well as outlets for independent authors like myself. I also wish to thank the "beta readers" whom I found through the Association, fellow independent authors who offered their comments and edits that greatly enhanced my drafts. The were Evan McMurry, Judith Reveal, Ken Lynch Leonard, Ken Stepanuk, and Barbra Morrison.

Finally, I wish to thank family members, friends, and colleagues who have sustained me through the long hours of researching, writing, editing, and publishing that have gone into this work. I am grateful to Jordan Diane McCalla and Zachary Ian McCalla, my daughter and son-in-law, who have read my works, have commented constructively on them, and have provided me with the often-necessary diversions from it that have kept me sane and healthy throughout. I am also grateful to Judith Cabaud and her family, my aunt and cousins in France, whose enormous talents and intelligence have been a constant source of inspiration to me.

Edgewater, Maryland

August 2024

ENDNOTES

[1] Doris Kearns Goodwin, *Team of Rivals* 115 (2005).

[2] Wikipedia.org, *Cornish, New Hampshire* (last viewed 1/3/2024); *Salmon P. Chase* (last viewed 1/3/2024).

[3] Jacob William Schuckers, *The Life of Salmon Portland Chase, United States Senator and Governor of Ohio* 3 (1874) (hereafter *Life of Chase*).

[4] *Life of Chase*, at 7.

[5] *Id.* at 8.

[6] *Id.* at 7.

[7] *Id.* at 8.

[8] *Id.* at 8.

[9] *Id.* at 9.

[10] *Id.* at 10.

[11] *Id.* at 10.

[12] *Id.* at 10-12.

[13] *Id.* at 13.

[14] *Id.* at 13.

[15] *Id.* at 15.

[16] *Id.* at 15.

[17] *Id.* at 15-16.

[18] *Id.* at 16.

[19] *Id.* at 16.

[20] *Id.* at 16.

[21] *Id.* at 16.

[22] *Id.* at 16.

[23] *Id.* at 16.

[24] *Id.* at 17.

[25] *Id.* at 17.

[26] *Id.* at 18.

[27] *Id.* at 18-19.

[28] *Id.* at 19.

[29] *Id.* at 20.

[30] *Id.* at 21.

[31] *Id.* at 22.

[32] *Id.* at 22-23.

[33] *Id.* at 23-24.

[34] *Id.* at 25 n.1.

[35] *Id.* at 25.

[36] *Id.* at 26.

[37] *Id.* at 27.

[38] *Id.* at 27; Teaching Matters, *The Arrest of Gilbert Horton and the Rise of the Abolition Movement (Part 1)*, https://davea.substack.com/p/the-arrest-of-gilbert-horton-and (last viewed 1/9/2024) (hereafter *Teaching Matters*).

[39] *Teaching Matters.*

[40] Wikipedia.org, *John Jay* (last viewed 1/9/2024).

[41] *Teaching Matters.*

[42] *Id.*

[43] *Life of Chase*, at 27.

[44] *Id.* at 28.

[45] *Id.* at 30.

[46] *Id.* at 30.

[47] *See id.* at 32-33 n.1 (Chase's September 17, 1830 letter to his brother Edwin).

[48] *Id.* at 35 n.1.

[49] John Niven, *Salmon P. Chase, A Biography* 39 (1995) (hereafter *Biography*).

[50] *Id.* at 31.

[51] *Id.* at 31.

[52] *Id.* at 31.

[53] *Id.* at 31.

[54] *Id.* at 32.

[55] *Life of Chase*, at 34; *Biography*, at 32.

[56] *Id.* at 34.

[57] *Id.* at 35.

[58] *Id.* at 37.

[59] *Biography*, at 40-41.

[60] *Id.* at 41.

[61] *Id.* at 41-42.

[62] *Id.* at 42.

[63] *Id.* at 43.

[64] *Id.* at 50.

[65] *Id.* at 71.

[66] *Id.* at 75.

[67] *Id.* at 76.

[68] *Id.* at 76.

[69] *Id.* at 103.

[70] Wikipedia.org, *Fugitive Slave Act of 1850* (last viewed 1/13/2024).

[71] *Life of Chase*, at 39.

[72] *Id.* at 40.

[73] *Id.* at 41; *Biography*, at 50.

[74] *Id.* at 41-42; *Biography*, at 50-51.

[75] *Biography*, at 51.

[76] *Id.* at 50; *Life of Chase*, at 41.

[77] *Biography*, at 51; *Life of Chase*, at 41-42.

[78] *Id.* at 51.

[79] *Id.* at 50; *Life of Chase*, at 41-42.

[80] Wikipedia.org, *James G. Birney* (last viewed 1/15/2024). Since 1896, the College of New Jersey has been known as Princeton University.

[81] http://famousamericans.net/davidkirkpatrickeste/ (last viewed 1/15/2024).

[82] *Biography*, at 51-52.

[83] *Somerset v. Stewart*, (1772) 98 Eng. Rep. 499 (KB) (hereafter *Somerset*).

[84] *Id.* at 510.

[85] *Biography*, at 52.

[86] *Id.* at 53.

[87] *Id.* at 54.

[88] *Id.* at 54.

[89] *Id.* at 56-57.

[90] *Life of Chase*, at 52.

[91] Randy E. Barnett, *From Antislavery Lawyer to Chief Justice: The Remarkable but Forgotten Career of Salmon P. Chase*, 63 Case W. Rsrv. L. Rev. 653, 662 (2013) (hereafter *Barnett*).

[92] *Id.* at 662.

[93] *Id.* at 668.

[94] *Id.* at 668.

[95] *Id.* at 669.

[96] *Id.* at 673.

[97] *Id.* at 673.

[98] Wikipedia.org, *Slavery Abolition Act 1833* (last viewed 1/29/2024).

[99] U.S. CONST., Art. I, § 9, cl. 1.

[100] Wikipedia.org, *End of slavery in the United States* (last viewed 1/29/2024).

[101] Wikipedia.org, *Cotton gin* (last viewed 1/29/2024).

[102] Wikipedia.org, *Stephen Duncan* (last viewed 1/30/2024).

[103] Edwin Earle Sparks, *The Lincoln-Douglas Debates* 52-53 (1918).

[104] *Id.* at 55 (1918).

[105] *Biography,* at 111-12.

[106] Benjamin Barondess, *Lincoln's Cooper Institute Speech* 4 (1953) (hereafter "*Lincoln's Cooper Speech*").

[107] *Id.* at 4-5.

[108] *Biography*, at 215.

[109] *Lincoln's Cooper Speech*, at 11.

[110] *Id.* at 11.

[111] *Id.* at 11.

[112] *Id.* at 12.

[113] *Id.* at 12.

[114] *Id.* at 12.

[115] *Id.* at 13.

[116] *Id.* at 13.

[117] *Id.* at 13-14.

[118] *NATIONAL POLITICS, A Speech Delivered at the Cooper Institute Last Evening, by ABRAHAM LINCOLN, of Illinois,* New York Daily Tribune, Feb. 28, 1860, at 6.

[119] *Biography*, at 215-16.

[120] Wikipedia.org, *1860 United States presidential election* (last viewed 2/19/2024).

[121] Wikipedia.org, *1860 United States presidential election* (last viewed 2/19/2024).

[122] *Life of Chase*, at 198 n.1.

[123] *Id.* at 198.

[124] *Id.* at 199.

[125] *Id.* at 199.

[126] *Id.* at 200.

[127] *Id.* at 201-03.

[128] *Id.* at 203.

[129] *Id.* at 203.

[130] *Id.* at 203-04.

[131] *Id.* at 203-04.

[132] *Id.* at 203-04.

[133] Wikipedia.org, *Peace Conference of 1861* (last viewed 3/2/2024).

[134] *How the South Rejected Compromise in the Peace Conference of 1861. Speech of Mr. Chase, of Ohio*, at 1-2 (Loyal Publication Society) (hereafter *Chase Peace Conf. Speech*).

[135] *Id.* at 5.

[136] *Id.* at 6.

[137] *Id.* at 6.

[138] *Id.* at 6-7.

[139] *Id.* at 8.

[140] *Id.* at 9.

[141] *Id.* at 10.

[142] *Id.* at 11.

[143] *Id.* at 11.

[144] *Life of Chase*, at 206.

[145] Harry Searles, *Washington Peace Conference of 1861*, American History Central (last viewed 3/3/2024).

[146] *Life of Chase*, at 207-08.

[147] John Niven, *Salmon P. Chase, A Biography* 241 (1995) (hereafter *Chase Biography*).

[148] U.S. Dept. of the Treasury, *Salmon P. Chase Suite*, https://home.treasury.gov/about/history/the-treasury-building/salmon-p-chase-suite (last viewed 3/9/2024).

[149] *Life of Chase*, at 212-13.

[150] *Id.* at 209.

[151] *Id.* at 209.

[152] *Id.* at 210.

[153] *Id.* at 210.

[154] *Id.* at 210.

[155] *Id.* at 210 n.1.

[156] *Id.* at 212.

[157] Eisenhower, John S.D., *Agent of Destiny: The Life and Times of General Winfield Scott* 349-52 (1999).

[158] Wikipedia.org, *Virginia Secession Convention of 1861* (last viewed 3/14/2024).

[159] *Life of Chase*, at 212-13.

[160] *Id.* at 213.

[161] *Id.* at 213.

[162] *Id.*, at 248.

[163] *Chase Biography*, at 248-49.

[164] *Id.*, at 249.

[165] *Id.*, at 249.

[166] *Life of Chase*, at 213.

[167] *Chase Biography*, at 251.

[168] Allan Nevins, *Abram S. Hewitt with Some Account of Peter Cooper* 49-55 (1935) (hereafter *Nevins*).

[169] *Id.* at 56.

[170] *Id.*, at 57.

[171] *Id.*, at 57-58.

[172] *Id.*, at 58-59.

[173] *Id.*, at 59-60.

[174] *Id.*, at 64-71.

[175] *Id.*, at 71-72.

[176] *Id.* at 73. Editor's note: This amounts to $15,357,218.57 in 2024 dollars.

[177] *Id.* at 281-82.

[178] *Id.* at 282.

[179] Wikipedia.org, *Edward Kellogg (economist)* (last viewed 3/17/2024).

[180] *Nevins*, at 282.

[181] Wikipedia.org, *Edward Kellogg (economist)* (last viewed 3/17/2024).

[182] *Nevins*, at 283-84.

[183] *Chase Biography*, at 249.

[184] *Id.*, at 250.

[185] Wikipedia.org, *United States Congress* (last viewed 3/19/2024) (chart showing party control of U.S. Senate and House of Representatives, 1855-2025).

[186] *Life of Chase*, at 214.

[187] *Id.* at 214-15.

[188] *Id.* at 215-16.

[189] *Id.* at 215-16.

[190] *Id.* at 216.

[191] *Id.* at 217.

[192] *Id.* at 217.

[193] *Id.* at 217.

[194] *Id.* at 217.

[195] *Id.* at 218.

[196] *Id.* at 219.

[197] *Id.* at 220.

[198] *Id.* at 220.

[199] *Id.* at 221.

[200] *Id.* at 221.

[201] *Id.* at 221.

[202] *Id.* at 222.

[203] *Id.* at 222.

[204] *Id.* at 222-23.

[205] Steven R. Weisman, *The Great Tax Wars* 40-42 (2002), https://archive.org/details/greattaxwars00weis .

[206] Wikipedia.org, *First Battle of Bull Run* (last viewed on 3/24/2024).

[207] *Id.*

[208] *Id.*

[209] *Id.*

[210] *Id.*

[211] *Life of Chase*, at 224.

[212] *Id.* at 224.

[213] *Id.* at 224-25.

[214] Howard Bodenhorn, *Open Access: Banks and Politics in New York from the Revolution to the Civil War* 11 (NBER June 2017) (hereafter *"Bodenhorn"*).

[215] *Id.* at 10.

[216] Drawing of New York Custom House, Wall Street, courtesy of Internet Archive Book Images (last viewed 3/25/2024).

[217] *Bodenhorn*, at 36.

[218] *Id.* at 36.

[219] *Life of Chase*, at 226 n.2.

[220] *Id.* at 229.

[221] *Id.* at 232.

[222] *Id.* at 227.

[223] Wikipedia.org, *Benjamin Butler* (last viewed 3/26/2024).

[224] *Life of Chase*, at 232.

[225] *Id.* at 227.

[226] *Id.* at 228, 232.

[227] *Id.* at 231.

[228] *Id.* at 233.

[229] U.S. CONST., Art. 1, § 10, cl. 1 ("No State shall ... make any Thing but gold and silver Coin a Tender in Payment of Debts....").

[230] U.S. CONST., Art. 1, § 8, cl. 5 ("The Congress shall have Power ... To Coin Money, [and] regulate the Value thereof....").

[231] *Nevins*, at 284-85.

[232] Wikipedia.org, *National Bank Act* (last viewed 4/6/2024).

[233] *Id.*

[234] *Life of Chase*, at 240-41.

[235] *Id.* at 242.

[236] *Id.* at 238.

[237] *Id.* at 236-37.

[238] *Id.* at 236-37.

[239] *Id.* at 239.

[240] *Biography*, at 297.

[241] *Life of Chase*, at 243 n.2.

[242] U.S. CONST., Art. I, §7, cl. 1.

[243] *Life of Chase*, at 243-44 n. 2.

[244] *Id.* at 248-49.

[245] U.S. Dept. of Treasury, *Salmon-Chase-Photo* (last viewed 4/8/2024).

[246] *Biography*, at 300.

[247] Wikipedia.org, *National Bank Act* (last viewed 4/13/2024).

[248] *Hepburn v. Griswold*, 75 U.S. 603, 619 (1869).

[249] *Life of Chase*, at 252.

[250] *Biography*, at 299.

[251] Wikipedia.org, *Confederate States of America* (last viewed 4/13/2024).

[252] *Biography*, at 292.

[253] *Id.* at 285.

[254] *Id.* at 286.

[255] *Id.* at 286.

[256] *Id.* at 299.

[257] *Id.* at 287.

[258] *Id.* at 286-87.

[259] *Id.* at 288.

[260] *Id.* at 289.

[261] *Id.* at 293.

[262] *Id.* at 294.

[263] *Id.* at 294.

[264] *Id.* at 294-95.

[265] *Id.* at 295.

[266] *Id.* at 295-96.

[267] *Id.* at 296.

[268] *Id.* at 303.

[269] *Id.* at 304.

[270] *Id.* at 304.

[271] *Id.* at 304.

[272] Wikipedia.org, *Emancipation Proclamation* (last viewed 4/24/2024).

[273] *Biography*, at 307.

[274] *Id.* at 308.

[275] *Id.* at 310.

[276] *Id.* at 310-11.

[277] *Id.* at 311.

[278] *See id.* at 312.

[279] *Id.* at 331.

[280] *Id.* at 331.

[281] Wikipedia.org, *Port Royal Experiment* (last viewed 4/29/2024).

[282] *Biography*, at 323-27.

[283] *Id.* at 328.

[284] *Id.* at 332.

[285] *Id.* at 332.

[286] *Id.* at 323.

[287] *Id.* at 340.

[288] *Id.* at 342-43.

[289] *Id.* at 357, 359-60.

[290] *Id.* at 360-61.

[291] *Id.* at 361.

[292] *Id.* at 361.

[293] *Id.* at 361-62.

[294] *Id.* at 363.

[295] *Id.* at 365.

[296] *Id.* at 366.

[297] *Life of Chase*, at 256.

[298] *Biography*, at 370.

[299] *Id.* at 370.

[300] *Id.* at 373.

[301] Wikipedia.org, *Salmon P. Chase* (last viewed May 9, 2024).

[302] Wikipedia.org, *Judicial Circuits Act* (last viewed May 9, 2024).

[303] Wikipedia.org, *Greenback (1860s money)* (last viewed May 10, 2024).

[304] *Id.*

[305] *Life of Chase*, at 258.

[306] U.S. CONST., Art I, §8, cl. 5 (emphasis added).

[307] U.S. CONST., Art I, §10, cl. 1.

[308] Wikipedia.org, *Greenback (1860s money)* (last viewed May 10, 2024).

[309] THE FEDERALIST No. 44, at 281-82 (James Madison) (Clinton Rossiter ed., 1961).

[310] *Hepburn v. Griswold*, 75 U.S. (8 Wall.) 603, 604 (1869) (hereinafter *"Hepburn"*).

[311] *Id.* at 605.

[312] *Id.* at 605.

[313] *Id.* at 605.

[314] *Id.* at 606-07 and fn. 2 and 3, citing *Lane County v. Oregon*, 74 U.S. (7 Wall.) 71 (1868); *Bronson v. Rodes*, 74 U.S. (7 Wall.) 229 (1868); and *Butler v. Horwitz*, 74 U.S. (7 Wall.) 258 (1868).

[315] *Hepburn*, at 607.

[316] *Cummings v. Missouri*, 71 U.S. (4 Wall.) 277; *Ex parte Garland*, 71 U.S. (4 Wall.) 333 (1866).

[317] U.S. CONST., Art. I, § 9, cl. 3.

[318] *Lane County v. Oregon*, 74 U. S. (7 Wall.) 71; *Bronson v. Rodes*, 74 U. S. (7 Wall.) 229; *Butler v. Horuitz*, 74 U. S. (7 Wall.) 258 (1868).

[319] U.S. CONST., Art. I, § 8, cl. 18.

[320] *McCullough v. Maryland*, 17 U. S. (4 Wheat.) 316, 421 (1819).

[321] *Id.* at 423 (1819).

[322] U.S. CONST., Art. I, § 8, cl. 5.

[323] *Id.*

[324] U.S. CONST., Art. I, § 8, cl. 2.

[325] National Constitution Center Staff, *Why the Supreme Court starts on the first Monday in October*, https://constitutioncenter.org/blog/why-the-supreme-court-starts-on-the-first-monday-in-october (October 2, 2023) (last viewed May 11, 2024).

[326] *Life of Chase*, at 266.

[327] *Hepburn*, at 607-08.

[328] *Id.* at 608.

[329] *Id.* at 610.

[330] *Id.* at 614.

[331] *Id.* at 614.

[332] *Id.* at 615.

[333] *Id.* at 616.

[334] *Id.* at 616.

[335] *Id.* at 616.

[336] *Id.* at 617.

[337] *Id.* at 618.

[338] *Id.* at 619.

[339] *Id.* at 620.

[340] *Id.* at 621.

[341] *Id.* at 621.

[342] *Id.* at 621.

[343] *Id.* at 622-23.

[344] *Id.* at 623.

[345] *Id.* at 627 (Miller, J., dissenting).

[346] *Id.* at 628 (Miller, J., dissenting).

[347] *Id.* at 628-31 (Miller, J., dissenting).

[348] *Id.* at 630-31 (Miller, J., dissenting), quoting *McCullough v. Maryland*, 17 U.S. (4 Wheat.) at 316.

[349] *Id.* at 633 (Miller, J., dissenting).

[350] *Id.* at 633-34 (Miller, J., dissenting).

[351] *Id.* at 626.

[352] *Life of Chase*, at 260-61.

[353] *Hepburn*, at 625-26.

[354] *Latham's and Deming's Appeals*, 76 U.S. (9 Wall.) 145 (1870).

[355] *Life of Chase*, at 262.

[356] *Id.* at 263.

[357] *Latham's and Deming's Appeals*, 76 U.S. (9 Wall.) 145 (1870).

[358] *Legal Tender Cases*, 79 U.S. 457 (1870).

[359] *Id.* at 457-59.

[360] *Id.* at 530.

[361] *Id.* at 533, quoting *Cohens v. Bank of Virginia*, 19 U.S. (6 Wheaton) 264, 414 (1821).

[362] *Id.* at 534.

[363] *Id.* at 540.

[364] *Id.* at 541-42.

[365] *Id.* at 544.

[366] *Id.* at 545.

[367] *Id.* at 546 (italics added).

[368] *Id.* at 548.

[369] *Id.* at 552.

[370] *Id.* at 553.

[371] *Id.* at 553-54.

[372] *Id.* at 294 (Chase, C.J., dissenting).

[373] *Id.* at 296 (Chase, C.J., dissenting).

[374] *Id.* at 298 (Chase, C.J., dissenting).

[375] *Id.* at 303 (Chase, C.J., dissenting).

[376] *Id.* at 303 (Chase, C.J., dissenting).

[377] *Id.* at 303 (Chase, C.J., dissenting).

[378] *Id.* at 305 (Chase, C.J., dissenting).

[379] *Id.* at 308-09 (Chase, C.J., dissenting).

[380] *Biography*, at 440.

[381] *Id.* at 444.

[382] *Id.* at 444.

[383] *Id.* at 443.

[384] *Id.* at 449.

[385] Wikipedia.org, *Cross of Gold Speech* (last viewed June 26, 2024).

[386] *Legal Tender Cases*, at 533, quoting *Cohens v. Bank of Virginia*, 19 U.S. (6 Wheaton) 264, 414 (1821).

[387] *United States v. Rahimi*, No. 22-915, slip op. at 7 (U.S., decided June 21, 2024) (citations omitted).

[388] *See* Stephanie Kelton, *The Deficit Myth* 15-40 (Hachette Book Group, Inc. 1st Trade Paperback ed. 2021).

[389] *Id.* at 19.

[390] *Id.* at 19.

[391] U.S. CONST., Amend. XIV, sec 4.

[392] Wikipedia.org, *Trillion-dollar Coin* (last viewed August 6, 2024).

Also by Steven Glazer

The Tenth Seat: A Novel
To The Victor
Greenback

About the Author

Steven A. Glazer is a retired lawyer and Administrative Law Judge who practiced in Washington, D.C. for 46 years. A graduate of M.I.T. with degrees in Economics and Civil Engineering, Steve now lives in Edgewater, Maryland, on the Chesapeake Bay next to Annapolis, and writes historical fiction novels.